PAN

Knut Hamsun was born in 1859 to a poor peasant family in central Norway. His early literary ambition was thwarted by having to eke out a living—as a schoolmaster, sheriff's assistant, and road laborer in Norway, as a store clerk, farmhand, and streetcar conductor in the American Midwest, where he lived for two extended periods between 1882 and 1888. Based on his own experiences as a struggling writer, Hamsun's first novel, *Sult* (1890; tr. *Hunger*, 1899), was an immediate critical success. While also a poet and playwright, Hamsun made his mark on European literature as a novelist. Finding the contemporary novel plot-ridden, psychologically unsophisticated and didactic, he aimed to transform it so as to accommodate contingency and the irrational, the nuances of conscious and subconscious life as well as the vagaries of human behavior. Hamsun's innovative aesthetic is exemplified in his successive novels of the decade: *Mysteries* (1892), *Pan* (1894), and *Victoria* (1898). Perhaps his best-known work is *The Growth of the Soil* (1917), which earned him the Nobel Prize in 1920. After the Second World War, as a result of his openly expressed Nazi sympathies during the German occupation of Norway, Hamsun forfeited his considerable fortune to the state. He died in poverty in 1952.

Sverre Lyngstad, Distinguished Professor Emeritus of English and Comparative Literature at New Jersey Institute of Technology, Newark, New Jersey, holds degrees in English from the University of Oslo, the University of Washington, Seattle, and New York University. He is the author of many books and articles in the field of Scandinavian literature, including *Jonas Lie* (1977) and *Sigurd Hoel's Fiction* (1984); co-author of *Ivan Goncharov* (1971); and co-translator of Tolstoy's *Childhood, Boyhood, and Youth* (1968). Among his more recent translations from Norwegian are Knut Faldbakken's *Adam's Diary* (1988), Sigurd Hoel's *The Troll Circle* (1992) and *The Road to the World's End* (1995), and Knut Hamsun's *Rosa* (1997) and *Hunger* (1997). Dr. Lyngstad is the recipient of several grants, prizes, and awards, and has been honored with the Saint Olav Medal by the king of Norway. He is currently preparing a critical study of Knut Hamsun's novels.

PAN

FROM THE PAPERS OF
LIEUTENANT THOMAS GLAHN

———————

KNUT HAMSUN

TRANSLATED WITH AN
INTRODUCTION AND EXPLANATORY
AND TEXTUAL NOTES
BY SVERRE LYNGSTAD

PENGUIN BOOKS

PENGUIN BOOKS
Published by the Penguin Group
Penguin Putnam Inc., 375 Hudson Street,
New York, New York 10014, U.S.A.
Penguin Books Ltd, 27 Wrights Lane,
London W8 5TZ, England
Penguin Books Australia Ltd, Ringwood,
Victoria, Australia
Penguin Books Canada Ltd, 10 Alcorn Avenue,
Toronto, Ontario, Canada M4V 3B2
Penguin Books (N.Z.) Ltd, 182–190 Wairau Road,
Auckland 10, New Zealand
Penguin India, 210 Chiranjiv Tower,
43 Nehru Place, New Delhi, India, 11009

Penguin Books Ltd, Registered Offices:
Harmondsworth, Middlesex, England

First published in Penguin Books 1998

5   7   9   10   8   6   4

Originally published in Norway in 1894.

LIBRARY OF CONGRESS CATALOGING-IN-PUBLICATION DATA
Hamsun, Knut, 1859–1952.
[Pan.   English]
Pan : from the papers of Lieutenant Thomas Glahn / Knut Hamsun ; translated
with an introduction and explanatory and textual notes by Sverre Lyngstad.
p.   cm.—(Penguin twentieth–century classics)
ISBN 0 14 11.8067 6
I. Lyngstad, Sverre.   II. Title.   III. Series.
PT8950.H3P313   1998
839.8'236—dc21   98-11351

Printed in the United States of America
Set in Bembo
Designed by Alice Sorensen

CONTENTS

INTRODUCTION

The publication of Hamsun's breakthrough novel, *Sult*, in 1890 (*Hunger*, 1899) turned Hamsun into a literary luminary, soon to be recognized on the European continent as well as in Scandinavia. From 1891 onward, however, his star shone much less brightly for several years, a setback that was largely of his own making. In that year, he traveled from one Norwegian city to another giving a series of lectures in which, among other things, he singled out the leading contemporary Norwegian writers for scathing criticism. Ibsen was present at the lecture he gave in Kristiania (now Oslo) in October 1891, sitting impassively in the front row beside Edvard Grieg and his wife, while young Hamsun faulted him and his writer colleagues, Lie, Kielland, and Bjørnson, for having produced a literature woefully lacking in imagination and psychological sophistication. The lectures triggered a slew of nasty attacks on Hamsun, accusing him, among other things, of using Yankee methods to promote his own career. Most bitter to Hamsun, perhaps, was the excoriating review of his lectures by his old benefactor, Ola Thommessen, editor of the daily *Verdens Gang*. In the spring of 1893, Hamsun took his revenge with the publication of *Redaktør Lynge* (Editor Lynge), whose central character is an opportunistic newspaper editor modeled on Thommessen.

Neither this novel nor its immediate successor, *Ny jord* (1893; *Shallow Soil*, 1914), was well received. This was all the more discouraging, since *Mysterier* (1892; *Mysteries*, 1927), Hamsun's programmatic novel of the preceding year—his greatest in the opinion of many Hamsun critics—had been condemned as a piece of charlatanry in some quarters. In general, the period between the publication of *Hunger* in 1890 and that of *Pan* in November 1894 was one of deep frustration in Hamsun's life. His emotional state is reflected by his restless mode of life: moving back and forth between various small towns in Norway, between Copenhagen and a Danish island, then alternating between Norway and Paris, where he spent most of his time between 1893 and 1895. Financially, as shown by the letters to his publishers, his situation was equally precarious.

Hamsun's writing of *Pan* grew out of this situation of embroilment in controversy and alienation from his native country. In a letter from Paris at the end of October 1893 he writes: "My new book will be so beautiful; it takes place in Nordland, a quiet and red love story. There will be no polemics in it, just people under different skies."[1] Meanwhile, the writing went very poorly: "[I] get stuck as if I were the most stupid of men. Write today and trash it tomorrow, all the time,"[2] he writes in January 1894. Paris did not seem to provide the right atmosphere for his writing; in a letter to his German publisher of June 5, 1894, he says he was unable to work there.[3] The novel was completed in Kristiansand, Norway, where a bad case of seasickness had made him disembark on his way north. Since for him the main thing was to get "on Norwegian soil and hear the Norwegian language," he decided he might as well settle there for the time being.[4] But while getting back to Norway may have stimulated the process of writing, the literary quality of the end result was no doubt partly due to the chosen subject and setting, which took the author on a sentimental journey beyond the Arctic Circle, to the region where he had spent his childhood and early youth. *Pan*, called by the contemporary critic Carl Nærup Hamsun's "great triumph,"[5] can be seen as the future Nobel laureate's second, and decisive, breakthrough as a novelist.

Hamsun's critical successes, first with *Hunger* and next with *Pan*, had not come cheaply. His beginnings as a writer had been slow and painful. By the time he appeared on the literary scene with a fragment of *Hunger* in 1888, he had served a literary apprenticeship of more than ten years and experienced life on two continents. That life, never an easy one, was often marked by severe hardship. Born to an impoverished peasant family at Garmotrædet, Lom, in central Norway in 1859, Knut Pedersen, to use his baptismal name, had a difficult childhood. In the summer of 1862, when Knut was less than three years old, his father, a tailor, moved with his family to Hamarøy, north of the Arctic Circle, where he worked the farm Hamsund belonging to his brother-in-law, Hans Olsen. From nine to fourteen Hamsun was a sort of indentured servant to his uncle, since the family was financially dependent on him. The boy's beautiful penmanship made him particularly valuable to Hans Olsen, who suffered from palsy and needed a scribe for his multifarious business, from shopkeeper to librarian and postmaster. The uncle treated him rather cruelly; he would rap his knuckles with a long ruler at the slightest slip of the pen. And on Sundays the boy had to sit indoors reading edifying literature to Hans and his pietist brethren, while his friends were outside waiting for him. No wonder Knut loved tending the parson's cattle, which allowed him to lie on his back in the woods dreaming his time away and writing on the sky. Very likely, these hours of solitary musings far from the tyranny of his uncle acted as a stimulus to young Hamsun's imagination. His schooling, starting at the age of nine, was sporadic, and his family had no literary culture. However, the local library at his uncle's place may have provided a modicum of sustenance for his childish dreams.

During his adolescence and youth Hamsun led a virtually nomadic existence, at first in various parts of Norway, later in the United States. After being confirmed in the church of his native parish in 1873, he was a store clerk in his godfather's business in Lom for a year, then returned north to work in the same capacity for Nikolai Walsøe, a merchant at Tranøy not far from his parents' place. There Hamsun seems to have fallen in love with the boss's daughter, Laura. It is uncertain whether the young man was asked to leave because of his infatuation with Laura or because of the bankruptcy of Mr. Walsøe in 1875. In the next few years he supported himself as a peddler, shoemaker's apprentice, schoolmaster, and sheriff's assistant in different parts of Nordland. After the failure of his literary ventures in the late 1870s, the school of life took the form of road construction work for a year and a half (1880–81).

Hamsun's dream of becoming a writer had been conceived at an early age, amid circumstances that gave him no choice but to fend for himself. If it can be said of any writer that he was self-made or self-taught, it can certainly be said of Hamsun. Not surprisingly, the two narratives published in his teens, *Den Gådefulde* (1877; The Enigmatic One) and *Bjørger* (1878), were clumsy and insignificant. The former is an idyllic tale in the manner of magazine fiction, in a language more Danish than Norwegian. The latter, a short novel, was modeled on Bjørnstjerne Bjørnson's peasant tales of the 1850s. In 1879, with the support of a prosperous Nordland businessman, E.B.K. Zahl, Hamsun wrote another novel, "Frida," which he presented to Frederik Hegel at Gyldendal Publishers in Copenhagen. It was turned down without comment. The manuscript of this story —which was dismissed by Bjørnson (1832–1910), Hamsun's idol, as well—has been lost. Bjørnson suggested he become an actor. And so, in early 1880, shortly after his twentieth birthday, the first period of Hamsun's literary apprenticeship came to an end.

The 1880s were marked by hard physical labor and renewed literary efforts. During the period he was employed in highway construction, he made his debut as a public lecturer. His next decision was not unusual for a poor, ambitious Norwegian in the 1880s: to emigrate to America. However, Hamsun's ambition was not chiefly to improve his fortune; instead, he foresaw a future for himself as the poetic voice of the Norwegian community in the New World. Needless to say, the dream quickly foundered, though the lecturing activity was continued. To support himself he worked as a farm hand and store clerk,

except for the last six months or so of his two-and-a-half-years'
stay, when he was offered the job of "secretary and assistant
minister with a salary of $500 a year" by the head of the Nor-
wegian Unitarian community in Minneapolis, Kristofer Janson
(1841–1917).[6] This was Hamsun's first significant encounter
with an intellectual milieu. While he did not share Janson's
religious beliefs, he clearly enjoyed browsing in his well-
stocked library. But his stay was cut short: in the summer of
1884 his doctor diagnosed "galloping consumption," and in the
fall of that year Hamsun returned to Norway, apparently resigned to die. He was twenty-five years old. His illness turned
out to be a severe case of bronchitis.[7]

Back in Norway, Hamsun's endeavors to support himself by
writing stories, articles and reviews for the newspapers, while
working on a "big book,"[8] brought only a meager harvest financially, despite a considerable amount of publishing activity.
Worthy of mention is his article on Mark Twain in the weekly
paper *Ny illustreret Tidende* (New Illustrated Gazette) in March
1885, important because by a compositor's error the "d" in his
name, Hamsund, was dropped. The young aspiring writer
adopted this spelling of his name for the rest of his life.

After a couple of years in Norway, at times in severe want,
he returned to America, but now for purely economic reasons:
to finance his literary ambition. From New York he wrote to
a friend in Norway that it had become "impossible" for him
at home.[9] However, the challenges posed by America were still
formidable. Only toward the end of his two-year stay, after
supporting himself as a streetcar conductor in Chicago and a
farm laborer in the Dakotas, was he able to turn his attention
to literature. Having returned to Minneapolis in the fall of
1887, he delivered a series of lectures there during the winter
of 1887–88. These lectures, which dealt with such literary figures as Balzac, Flaubert, Zola, Bjørnson, Ibsen and Strindberg,
demonstrate Hamsun's painfully acquired familiarity with the
literary culture of his time. By July 1888 we find him in Co-

penhagen. In a brief sketch of his early life recorded in 1894 he says he "hid on board a day and a half"[10] when the ship reached Kristiania, bypassing the city that had so bitterly frustrated his literary dreams. In early November 1888 the above-mentioned fragment of his breakthrough novel, *Hunger*, was published in the Danish journal *Ny jord* (New Earth), and Hamsun's literary career had truly gotten started.

The controversial lectures that Hamsun gave in 1891 contained a broadside attack on the traditional novel, accusing it of applying a superficial psychology and showing a utilitarian concern with social problems. Furthermore, they derided what he called literary creation by dint of "science and numbers," stressing that an author is a "subjectivity" whose depiction of life and people flows from his own feelings.[11] In particular Hamsun criticized the work of his elders for its allegedly stereotypic character portrayal, expressing a preference for the changeable and divided mind, for individuals "in whom inconsistency is literally their fundamental trait."[12] He wants to see the "soul illuminated and scrutinized every way, from all viewpoints, in every secret recess"; "I will," he says, "transfix its vaguest stirring on my pin and hold it up to my magnifying glass," prepared to examine "the most delicate vibrations." Significantly, the emphasis on emotional nuances also includes a preference for depicting mental phenomena in a state of becoming: he wants to direct attention to the "first germ" of thought and feeling rather than the "final bud" or flower. This accounts for his relative neglect of external action, since elements of plot—balls, outings, and so forth—show nothing but *the result* of a psychic process rather than that process "in its first germ and its unfolding." "Thoughts," he says, "rise and change at the slightest impressions, and decisions and actions ripen by means of thoughts."[13]

Hamsun's intent in writing *Pan* is quite consistent with this program, which he had failed to follow in his two immediately

preceding novels, *Editor Lynge* and *Shallow Soil*. In a letter written after its publication, he says that he "wrote *Pan* for the
sake of the changing emotions, nothing but reflexes. . . ."[14]
Another letter goes even further, declaring that Glahn himself
"is supposed to be a bundle of changing emotions, soul,
rising and sinking moods."[15] To give Albert Langen, his German publisher, an idea of the book, he asks him to "think of
J. J. Rousseau" in the region of Nordland—with its Lapps, its
"mysteries," its "grand superstitions" and its midnight sun—
making the acquaintance of a local girl. He says he is trying to
express "some of the nature-worshipping, sensitivity, over-
nervousness in a Rousseauian soul."[16] In another letter to Langen he writes that "every chapter is a poem. . . ."[17]

The actual work is obviously more complex than Hamsun's
plan suggests. The narrative situation appears deceptive, the
characters' behavior oftentimes excessively wayward, key incidents gratuitously gruesome. There is also the problem of
how to read "Glahn's Death," originally published in the journal *Samtiden* (The Contemporary) in 1893. Some Hamsun critics have opted to pay scant attention to the epilogue, which
presents a challenge to anyone who believes that a work of art
should be aesthetically unified. Partly as a result of these problems and idiosyncrasies, *Pan* has elicited a continuous flow of
articles as well as a book-length study,[18] signs of the continuing
vitality of Hamsun's Nordland story. For while the interpretations differ, in particular with regard to the major characters,
the novel has continued to exercise a kind of magic charm
upon readers and critics alike.

The main story of Thomas Glahn comes to us through a
retrospective narrative, something between a diary, a memoir,
and a meditation, by Glahn himself. In the intervening two
years between the time the events occurred and their being
committed to writing, he has led what he himself calls a
"merry" life in the city, most likely the capital. But now, with
the reception of two "devilishly green" bird's feathers—one of

several leitmotifs in the story—Glahn's involuntary memory will not let him rest. Given as a "remembrance" to Edvarda, the young woman he claims to have forgotten, the feathers seem to be present to the eyes and mind of Glahn as he records what he calls his "little joke" in Nordland. In the last chapter of his narrative, they even induce a near-hallucinatory experience: "And suddenly I seem to see a face and hear a voice, and the voice says, 'Please, Lieutenant, here are your feathers, Sir!' " His final protestations that he has "no regrets" and that he has been writing purely for his "own amusement" are no more convincing than his initial disclaimers of writing simply "to pass the time."

Early Hamsun critics apparently failed to detect the many telltale signs of an unreliable narrator in *Pan*. They envisaged Glahn as a romantic nature worshiper pure and simple and took his pantheistic feelings and lyrical effusions at their face value. Recent decades have produced a number of new interpretations of Glahn, ranging from psychopath[19] to artist to alienated modern man. In particular, commentators have come to regard Glahn's love of the wilderness as compensation for his social ineptitude and amorous frustrations. Carried to its logical extreme, the older view turned the novel into a paean to nature and eros, whereas the later one has uncovered a far more complex literary structure, permeated with ambiguities and ironies that are compounded by the epilogue, "Glahn's Death," which was largely ignored by the early critics.

In trying to understand Hamsun's *Pan*, it is important to remember that Glahn lives on the edge of the forest, at the point where wild nature and civilization meet. Somewhat of a "superfluous man" like his predecessors in the novels of Turgenev, he can find no meaningful place for himself in bourgeois society, and so he withdraws to the woods, to the state of nature. But so far, despite his "lair," his animal eyes, and his animal clothing, he lacks the natural completion that he longs for. Interestingly, in his 1888 article on August Strindberg,

Hamsun recalls Strindberg's description of himself as "an animal longing for the woods,"[20] before citing examples of modern man's attempt to return to his natural condition. The image of the Rousseauian Swede, who influenced Hamsun as much as anybody, may have been at the back of his mind when conceiving Lieutenant Glahn. While the impulse—whether of Strindberg, Hamsun, or Glahn—may have been authentic enough, Hamsun's hero gives us contradictory signals as to his true nature. Is he simply a disenchanted city man temporarily seeking refuge in the wilds (Glahn as tourist), or is he a self-deceived romantic who compensates for his social and sexual shortcomings and misadventures by a deliberate cult of nature (Glahn the false primitive)?

It is not easy to distinguish between the real and affected traits of Thomas Glahn. Though his "animal eyes" are attested to by several characters, in general Glahn gives the impression of being anything but animalistic: when he manages to preserve his self-control he behaves *comme il faut;* one need only think of his sense of shock when Edvarda (a more authentic primitive) kisses him on the lips during the first outing to the island (chapter X). He repeatedly regrets not having his uniform at hand, hoping it will help him regain Edvarda's favor. In view of these facts, his animal clothing and his "lair" hung with animal skins, together with his idea of being a true "son of the forest," become rather suspect. Nor is his feeling for nature that of a true primitive; in fact, it is sometimes so sentimental that it verges on the maudlin, such as licking the blades of grass and getting tears in his eyes from watching a nearly rotten little twig. These are signs of an oversensitive, nostalgic urban sensibility rather than of a primordial oneness with nature.

Even if one accepts Glahn's feeling for nature as genuine, his invocations and uses of nature prove contradictory. While he clearly enjoys initiating Edvarda into his simple woodsman's life, governed by nature's clock, subsequently nature comes to play an ambiguous role in their relationship. A crucial instance is seen near the end of chapter XIII, where Edvarda flings her arms around his neck, "breathing audibly," her eyes "quite black." She is obviously offering herself to him. His reason— or rationalization—for turning her down is revealing. When she asks him why he got up so quickly, he answers, "Because it's late, Edvarda. . . . Now the white flowers are closing again, the sun is rising, it'll soon be day." Here nature, in the form of the diurnal cycle, is used to justify his evasion of Edvarda's passionate appeal. And during the so-called Iron Nights (chapter XXVI), by which time he has pretty much given up on Edvarda, he stages a veritable ritual of exorcism, a self-induced mystical union with nature and nature's god that he hopes will liberate him from his passion. Eventually his relationship to nature turns paradoxical: the man capable of feeling friendly toward a rock eventually causes the death of Eva, a woman he claims to love, by means of a rock fragment released by his farewell salute to his rival, the Baron.

While nature helps Glahn evade human intimacy, it also compensates for the lack of such intimacy. He treats his dog, for example, as if he were a human being: feeling neglected by Edvarda during an outing, he tells the company repeatedly that Aesop, his friend, is waiting for him in the hut. In general, his anthropomorphic attitude toward nature creates a simulacrum of a human society in the midst of the forest, a society that allows his ego to expand to virtual infinity. Thus, in appealing to nature to fend off Edvarda's sexual advances, he eroticizes —and therefore humanizes—the very flowers that he invokes: the flowers "are steeped in an erotic ecstasy . . ." (chapter XIII). This eroticizing of nature cannot but ricochet back on Glahn's consciousness, inflating it so as to embrace the unconscious life of nature itself. The ultimate expression of this relationship is seen in the account of the third Iron Night, where Glahn describes what looks like his sexual union with the moon goddess: ". . . I feel myself lifted out of my sphere, pressed to an invisible breast, my eyes are moist with tears, I tremble. . . ." This experience of quasi-apotheosis confers a cosmic dimension upon Glahn's self through mythic identification.

The elements of myth, legend, and dream in Hamsun's *Pan* are central to our understanding of Glahn and of his relationship to the other characters, especially the women. Though the book's title seems to have come to Hamsun by way of a casual impulse in ending a letter to Albert Langen—the letter ends "Pan bless you!"[21]—the ramifications of the Pan myth seem important. They turn up at different levels of the text. On the most superficial level, Pan is present as a figurine on Glahn's powder horn, part and parcel of his gear as a woodsman. We are told that the Doctor "explains" the myth of Pan, but we are not provided with his explanation. It seems that Hamsun exploits the paradoxical duality of the goat-god's nature as god and animal in relation to his hero: though Glahn is said to have "animal" eyes, to Edvarda he looks "like a god" (end of chapter XXIII). More important, Pan combines the attributes of the primitive Arcadian god of fertility with those ascribed to him, by way of etymological confusion, by the Stoics and incorporated in the Orphic Hymn to Pan. According to this interpretation, Pan encompasses "the heavens, the sea, earth, and fire—universal Nature . . . , becoming Supreme Governor or 'soul' of the World."[22]

The Pan that Glahn fantasizes about in chapter VIII seems to be the primitive god of the woods, though the way he is imagined as "drinking from his own belly" and making the tree in which he sits shake with "his silent laughter," all the while keeping an eye on Glahn, strongly suggests that Glahn feels uncertain about his relationship to what the primitive god stands for. During the Iron Nights, however, it is the pantheistic Pan that Glahn experiences, a god "transfusing me and the world," as he writes. Chapter XXVI ends with the episode referred to above, where Glahn enacts the role of Pan in relation to the moon goddess, once ravished by the goat-god according to a tradition handed down by Virgil (*The Georgics*, III, 391–93).[23] But once more Glahn feels watched by God— by Pan? In any case, Glahn glimpses only what looks like the "back of a spirit wandering soundlessly through the forest," somewhat like Moses, who is vouchsafed to see only Yahweh's "back parts" (Exodus, 33:23).

While the Pan myth reinforces Glahn's ambivalent relationship to nature,[24] the legend of Iselin that Glahn conjures up immediately after the first "appearance" of Pan (chapter VIII) adumbrates his ideal of a free, amoral sexuality. But curiously, Iselin's surrender to the hunter occurs only to the detriment of an "injured third party," her husband, Diderik. This archetypal triangle shapes all the love relationships, real or imagined, in the novel: Diderik/Iselin/Glahn; Henriette's sweetheart/ Henriette/Glahn; Dundas/Iselin/Glahn; Mack/Eva/Glahn; the Doctor/Edvarda/Glahn; the Baron/Edvarda/Glahn; the narrator of "Glahn's Death"/Maggie/Glahn. While the use of the Iselin legend may suggest that Glahn desires an absolutely untrammeled, non-binding sexuality—a desire that seems to be promptly fulfilled by his docile partners, Henriette and Eva, after the two installments of the legend have been given (chapters VIII and XX, respectively)—his sexuality is no more unequivocable than his relationship to nature. Pure eroticism seems impossible; it invariably entails a power game, whatever its origin, whether in the laws of nature or in those of the society that he flouts. There will always be winners and losers. The anomalous situation in *Pan* is that practically everybody is a loser.

Traditionally, the Glahn/Edvarda relationship has been interpreted in tune with the above: their love falls prey either to a Strindbergian battle between the sexes or to the natural rhythms of the seasonal cycle. But unlike the amorous attraction that Glahn has for Henriette, the shepherdess, Edvarda's love for Glahn does not die, nor does Glahn's love for her; Edvarda's second letter clearly testifies to an enduring passion, as does Glahn's retrospective regret and existential despair. Glahn and Edvarda's love is not affected by naturalistic metaphysics; it is a passion love, an arctic variety of the alleged civilized malady examined by Denis de Rougemont in *L'Amour et l'Occident* (1939; *Love in the Western World*, 1957).[25] Comparable to the passion of Tristan for Isolde, Goethe's Werther for Lotte, and Heathcliff for Catherine in *Wuthering Heights*, Glahn's obsession with Edvarda is conditioned by distance,[26] by the impossibility of fulfillment—except in death. Significantly, Glahn dresses up like a bridegroom on the last morning of his life: Hamsun ends *Pan* with an extraordinary variation of the love-death motif. Glahn's sexual affairs are trivial by comparison: as he tells Eva, what he loves most is the dream, and that means the complex of transcendent sentiments associated with Edvarda.

In conceiving this love, in particular the suffering that it entails, Hamsun may have received a stimulus from Arthur Schopenhauer (1788–1860) and his philosophical heir Eduard von Hartmann (1842–1906), two proponents of pessimism whom Hamsun admired. The former writes, among other things, that passionate love is "the source of little pleasure and much suffering."[27] The latter, who developed a "philosophy of the unconscious," speaks of love as a "demon who ever and again demands his victim," and as an "eternally veiled mystery" that wills an infinitude of "longing, joy and sorrow"; it is "eternally incomprehensible, unutterable, ineffable, because never to be grasped by consciousness."[28] Already in 1890, Hamsun had published an article entitled "Fra det ubevidste Sjæleliv" (From the Unconscious Life of the Mind), in which he aimed to demonstrate the power of the unconscious in human behavior, thought, and creativity.[29]

Confronted with the archetype of passion love and with Hamsun's emphasis on the unconscious, one comes to feel that a too close analysis of why the characters behave as they do in the novel is pointless; they act as they must, often irrationally and self-destructively. No rational explanation can be found for the undying love of the maiden imprisoned in the tower (chapter XXXIII) or of Eva's steadfast love for Glahn. Nor can we find sufficient reasons for Glahn's eccentric, often self-destructive behavior—breaking his glass, throwing Edvarda's shoe overboard, shooting himself in the foot, expressing pleasure at the idea of being dragged by the hair, spitting in the Baron's ear.[30] The various theories—Dionysian, Freudian, Jungian—cannot quite pluck out the mystery of this book.

Suffice it to cite a deconstructive attempt by a Norwegian critic, Asmund Lien. Having discovered that the text contradicts itself, Professor Lien sees Glahn as a "masked modern intellectual" whose enactment of the role of a Rousseauian "tourist" in a primordial setting leads to disastrous consequences. The text shows, he says, that Glahn "knows" what he does when he triggers the rockfall, that he makes use of Mack's persecution of Eva to kill Eva, thus sacrificing her—as he does Aesop—to Edvarda.[31] Each reader will have to decide whether the work gains or loses by such an approach, namely, interpreting what looks like accidents or gratuitous acts as due to conscious calculation rather than to motives deliberately left obscure by the author.

What type of novel is *Pan*? The question would be more readily answerable if the story ended with Glahn's departure from Nordland. If Hamsun had decided not to include "Glahn's Death," the novel could be seen as a Scandinavian example of what Ralph Freedman has chosen to call a "lyrical novel." While Freedman does not give us a definition of the genre, he says that it "seeks to combine man and world in a strangely inward, yet aesthetically objective, form."[32] One of the prime examples he offers of this type of novel has already been mentioned, namely, Goethe's *Werther* (1774), with which *Pan* has much in common: an outsider hero to whom the world is largely a reflection of his moods, an ecstatic experience of nature that doesn't stop at mooning over leaves of grass, a sense of eros as an inexorable natural force, and a style that has many of the earmarks of poetry.[33] The "I" of the novel is as much lyrical as narrative, producing quasi-musical modulations of pace and rhythm: thus, the mythic and legendary sequences have a timeless quality, as does the evocation of nature in its various phases and moods. Moreover, the circular form, highlighted by the motif of the bird's feathers, has the effect of condensing the elapsed time: while the summer passes quickly and the brief chapters produce a rapid pace, for the narrator—and secondarily the reader—the story contracts to one haunting, eternally recurring moment.

Many critics have been puzzled by Hamsun's decision to add "Glahn's Death" to the novel. Once we realize that it is part and parcel of the text, our understanding of the work as a whole changes radically.[34] For while the lyrical novel is a traditional genre, however recent its critical investigation, the approximation to narrative montage resulting from the juxtaposition of Glahn's story with that of his hate-ridden hunting companion in India marks *Pan* as a distinctly modernistic work. The links between the two parts—the subjectivity of the narrators, the triangle situation, the exotic settings—cannot conceal the drastic change in style and tone: from the near-sentimental to the crass, from nature as a wellspring of sublime, religiously tinged emotions to deadly male rivalry in an arena of killing for sport, from all-consuming passion to tawdry, exploitative one-night stands.

The principal effect of the epilogue is to add another layer of irony to Hamsun's novel. We have seen that Glahn relates his story in such a way as to make him appear as an unreliable narrator; moreover, as an actor in the story he tells he may sometimes strike us as unnecessarily cruel. Yet, we do not therefore deny him our sympathy or compassion, largely because we realize that he is in the grip of utter despair and irremediable suffering. But it is difficult to sympathize with the colonial hunter avid for the kill that we are given in "Glahn's Death," unless we can persuade ourselves that his companion's "inside story" is fatally flawed, based on a murderous jealousy and therefore false. If we begin to suspect that Glahn is slandered, we may even feel like coming to his defense—until, perhaps, we recall that in many respects his own narrative was also rooted in jealousy. The upshot of these reflections is to further problematize the novel, whose meaning, in the final analysis, appears to be undecidable. It will be up to each individual reader to decide who Glahn is, what makes him act as he does, and how to respond to Hamsun's seductive, but perplexing story.

NOTES

1. Letter of October 31, 1893, to Bolette and Ole Johan Larsen, in *Knut Hamsuns brev*: I, ed. Harald S. Næss (Oslo: Gyldendal, 1994), 354. Hereafter cited as *Brev*. See also Knut Hamsun, *Selected Letters*: I, ed. Harald Næss and James McFarlane (Norwich, England: Norvik Press, 1990), 179. Hereafter cited as *Letters*.
2. Letter of January 4, 1894, to the Larsens, in *Brev*, 382.
3. Letter of June 5, 1894, to Albert Langen, in *Brev*, 412; *Letters*, 199.
4. Letter of June 15, 1894, to the Larsens, in *Brev*, 415; *Letters*, 203.
5. "Knut Hamsun," in *Skildringer og stemninger fra den yngre litteratur* (Kristiania, 1897), 49.
6. Letter of February 29, 1884, to Svend Tveraas, in *Brev*, 42; *Letters*, 42.
7. Harald Næss, *Knut Hamsun* (Boston: Twayne, 1984), 12.
8. Letter of January 19, 1886, to Nikolai Frøsland, in *Brev*, 63.
9. Letter of September 4, 1886, to Erik Frydenlund, in *Brev*, 69; *Letters*, 58.
10. Letter in November 1894 to the Larsens, in *Brev*, 431; *Letters*, 214.
11. "Psykologisk literatur," in *Paa Turné: Tre foredrag om litteratur*, ed. Tore Hamsun (Oslo: Gyldendal, 1960), 51.
12. Ibid., 66.
13. Ibid., 70–71.
14. Letter of September 23, 1895, to Marie Bregendahl, in *Brev*, 478.
15. Letter of January 11, 1895, to Elisa Philipsen, in *Brev*, 446.

INTRODUCTION xxiii

16. Letter of July 22, 1894, in *Brev*, 418; *Letters*, 205. Hamsun's English is rather nontraditional in its grammar and spelling.

17. Letter of September 2, 1894, to Albert Langen, in *Brev*, 422; *Letters*, 208.

18. Rolf Vige, *Knut Hamsuns "Pan": En litterær analyse* (Oslo: Universitetsforlaget, 1963).

19. In 1985 Knut Faldbakken published a novel, *Glahn*, which is a satiric reworking of Hamsun's *Pan* on a psychoanalytic basis. Interviewed by the author in 1986, Faldbakken said that he had wanted "to show Glahn up for the self-destructive psychopath that he is." See Sverre Lyngstad, "An Interview with Knut Faldbakken, Part II," *Norway Times*, September 17, 1987: 12

20. "August Strindberg," *America* (Chicago), I. 38 (December 20, 1888): 31.

21. Letter of September 2, 1894, to Albert Langen, in *Brev*, 423; *Letters*, 208.

22. Patricia Merivale, *Pan the Goat-God: His Myth in Modern Times* (Cambridge, Mass.: Harvard University Press, 1969), 9.

23. Robert Browning wrote a grotesque poem, "Pan and Luna," where he questions this tradition (*Dramatic Idylls, Second Series, The Poetical Works of Robert Browning* [London: Oxford University Press, 1946], 620–22).

24. For a comprehensive discussion of the function of the myth of Pan in the novel, see Henning K. Sehmsdorf, "Knut Hamsun's *Pan*: Myth and Symbol," *Edda* 74 (1974): 345–93.

25. Øystein Rottem has convincingly argued this view in "*Pan*—en høysang til kjærligheten eller Tusten i jegerkostyme," in Nils M. Knutsen, ed., *"Pan": Handelsstedene, novellene, illustrasjonene*. Rapport frå litteraturseminaret, Hamsundagene 1986 (Tromsø: Tromsø University Press, 1986), 9–44.

26. Thomas Seiler reads Glahn's need for distance as a sign that he is an artist whose creativity depends on the tension between distance and nearness. See "Knut Hamsuns *Pan* als patriarchaler Schöpfer-Mythos," *Edda* 95 (1995): 272.

27. "On the Sufferings of the World," in *Parerga and Paralipomena*, tr. T. Bailey Saunders, in K. Francke and W. G. Howard, eds., *The German Classics*, XV (New York, 1914), 84.

28. Eduard von Hartmann, *Philosophy of the Unconscious*, new one-volume ed., tr. W. C. Coupland and with a preface by C. K. Ogden (London: Routledge and Kegan Paul, 1931), 229–30.

29. In Knut Hamsun, *Artikler*, ed. Francis Bull (Oslo: Gyldendal, 1939), 46–63.

30. For several of these gratuitous acts, Hamsun may have received suggestions from Dostoyevsky. In *The Idiot* (Part IV, chapter 7), Myshkin's breaking of the china vase produces a typical Dostoyevskian scene of scandal; in *Crime and Punishment* (Part I, chapter 2), Marmeladov expresses pleasure in his wife's dragging him by the hair; and in *The Demons* (Part I, chapter 2, II), Stavrogin, pretending to whisper something in the governor's ear, bites it instead.

31. Asmund Lien, "Pans latter," *Edda* 93 (1993): 134–35.

32. *The Lyrical Novel: Studies in Hermann Hesse, André Gide, and Virginia Woolf* (Princeton, N. J.: Princeton University Press, 1963), 2.

33. In his article "Das Werther-Thema in Hamsuns 'Mysterien'," Frank Thiess sees *Pan* as well as *Mysteries* as exemplifying the Werther theme. See *Heimat und Weltgeist: Jahrbuch der Knut Hamsun-Gesellschaft*, ed. Hilde Fürstenberg (Mölln, Lauenberg, 1960), 151.

34. For a strongly argued presentation of this view, see Siegfried Weibel, "Knut Hamsuns *Pan*: Suggestion und De-Montage," *Skandinavistik* 16 (1986): 21–35.

SUGGESTIONS FOR FURTHER READING

Barksdale, E. C., and Daniel Popp. "Hamsun and Pasternak: The Development of Dionysian Tragedy." *Edda* 76 (1976): 343–51.

Buttry, Dolores. "The Friendly Stone: Hamsun's Pathetic Fallacy." *Edda* 79 (1979): 151–56.

Ferguson, Robert. *Enigma: The Life of Knut Hamsun.* New York: Farrar, Straus and Giroux, 1987.

Hamsun, Knut. *Rosa.* Trans. Sverre Lyngstad. Los Angeles: Sun and Moon Press, 1997.

Lavrin, Janko. "The Return of Pan." In *Aspects of Modernism.* London: S. Nott, 1935. Freeport, N.Y.: Books for Libraries Press, 1968. Pp. 93–111.

McFarlane, James W. "Knut Hamsun," in *Ibsen and the Temper of Norwegian Literature.* London: Oxford University Press, 1960). Pp. 114–57.

———. "The Whisper of the Blood: A Study of Knut Hamsun's Early Novels." *PMLA* 71 (1956): 563–94.

Mazor, Yair. "The Epilogue in Knut Hamsun's *Pan*," *Edda* 84 (1984): 313–28.

Næss, Harald. *Knut Hamsun.* Boston: Twayne, 1984.

———. "Strindberg and Hamsun." In *Structures of Influence: A Comparative Approach to August Strindberg*, ed. Marilyn Johns Blackwell. University of North Carolina Studies in Germanic Languages and Literatures 98. Chapel Hill, 1981. Pp. 121–36.

———. "Who Was Hamsun's Hero?" In *The Hero in Scandinavian Literature: From Peer Gynt to the Present.* Ed. John M. Weinstock and Robert T. Rovinsky. Austin: Texas University Press, 1975. Pp. 63–86.

Popperwell, Ronald. "Knut Hamsun and *Pan*." *Scandinavica* 25 (May 1986): 19–31.

Sehmsdorf, Henning K. "Knut Hamsun's *Pan*: Myth and Symbol." *Edda* 74 (1974): 345–93.

Sjåvik, Jan. "A New Psychological Novel, a New Narrative Technique, and Salvation through Art: Knut Hamsun's *Pan* and the Artist's Quest for Recognition." *Selecta: Journal of the Pacific Northwest Council on Foreign Languages* 4 (1983): 94–100.

Turco, Alfred. "Hamsun's *Pan* and the Riddle of 'Glahn's Death'." *Scandinavica* 19 (May 1980): 13–29.

TRANSLATOR'S NOTE

While the translation history of Hamsun's *Pan* (1894) is not as deplorable as that of *Hunger* (1890), the first version, by W. W. Worster (Knopf, 1921), was bowdlerized, all the expressly erotic elements, however innocuous, having been deleted. James W. McFarlane's rendering (Farrar, Straus & Giroux, 1956) is the work of a well-known English Hamsun scholar and translator. In an attempt to reproduce the tone of oral narrative so characteristic of *Pan*, the present translation hews as closely as possible to Hamsun's idiosyncratic syntax, punctuation, and rhythm. Special care has been taken to get the details of the flora and fauna of North Norway correct. The translator wishes to thank Dagfinn Worren of the University of Oslo for identifying several bird species of the region.

PAN

I

I've thought and thought, these last few days, about the endless day of the Nordland summer. I sit here and think about it, about a hut I lived in, and about the forest behind the hut, and I take to writing things down for my own amusement and to pass the time. Time hangs heavy, I can't make it pass as quickly as I would like, though I have no regrets and lead the merriest of lives. I'm quite content with everything, and thirty is no great age. A few days ago I received a pair of bird's feathers from far away, from someone who was under no obligation to send them to me—two green feathers in a sheet of letter paper with a coronet on it and sealed with a wafer. It gave me real pleasure to see those two feathers, so devilishly green. Otherwise I have no complaints, except for a touch of rheumatism in my left foot now and then, from an old gunshot wound that has long since healed.

Two years ago, I remember, time passed very quickly, more quickly by far than now; the summer was gone before I realized it. It was two years ago, in 1855—I'm going to write about it just to amuse myself—that something happened to me, or I dreamed it. By now I've forgotten many things that are part of those happenings, because I have hardly ever thought of them since; but I can remember that the nights were very light. Also, many things seemed to be so out of joint: the year had twelve months, but night became day and you never saw a star in the sky. And the people I met were peculiar and of a different nature than the people I used to know; sometimes a single night was enough to change them from child to adult, making them come out in all their glory,[1] mature and fully grown. There was nothing magical in this, I just hadn't seen anything like it before. No, I hadn't.

In a large white-painted house down by the sea I met some-

one who for a while occupied my thoughts. She is no longer
constantly in my thoughts, not now—no, I've quite forgotten
her; but I do think of all the other things, the cries of the sea
birds, going hunting in the woods, my nights, all the warm
hours of summer. Anyway, I got to know her by pure chance,
and if not for that chance she wouldn't have been in my
thoughts for a single day.

From my hut I could see a scattering of islands and rocks
and skerries, a bit of the sea, a few bluish peaks; and behind
the hut lay the forest, a vast forest. I was filled with joy and
gratitude at the fragrance of the roots and leaves and the fatty
odor of the pine, reminiscent of the smell of marrow; only in
the woods was all at rest within me, my soul became still and
full of power. Day after day I would walk in the hills with
Aesop at my side, and I wished for nothing better than being
allowed to continue walking there day after day, though the
ground was still half covered with snow and soft slush. My only
companion was Aesop; now there's Cora, but at that time I
had Aesop, my dog, whom I later shot.

In the evening when I returned to the hut after the hunt, I
would often feel a warm sense of home ripple through me from
top to toe, setting off sweet tremors in my heart, and I would
chat with Aesop about how well-off we were. "Come, now
we'll make a fire and roast ourselves a bird on the hearth," I
would say, "what do you say to that?" And when it was all
done and we had both eaten, Aesop crept over to his place
behind the hearth, while I would light a pipe and lie down on
my bed for a few moments and listen to the dead soughing of
the forest. There was a slight breeze, the wind bearing down
on the hut, and I could hear quite clearly the call of the blackcock far away in the hills. Other than that, all was quiet.

And many a time I fell asleep where I lay, fully clad, in my
togs, just as I was, and didn't awake until the sea birds had
started crying. Then, when I looked out the window, I could
catch a glimpse of the large white buildings of the trading cen-

ter, the piers of Sirilund, and the general store where I used to buy my bread, and I would lie there awhile, surprised to find myself in a hut at the edge of a forest in Nordland.

Then Aesop would shake his long, spare body over by the hearth, jingling his collar, yawning and wagging his tail, and I would jump up after my three or four hours' sleep, refreshed and rejoicing in everything, everything.

Thus passed many a night.

II

Rain or blow, no matter; often on a rainy day some little joy will take possession of you and make you steal away with your happiness. You stand there staring straight ahead, laughing softly now and then and looking around. What are you thinking of? A clear pane in some window, a ray of sunlight on the pane, the view of a small creek and perhaps a break of blue in the sky. It need be no more.

At other times even unusual experiences cannot jolt you out of a flat, impoverished mood; in the middle of a ballroom you may sit stolid and indifferent, unaffected by anything. For the source of grief or joy lies within.

I remember a certain day. I had gone down to the seaside. Surprised by the rain, I went into an open boathouse to sit for a while. I hummed a little, but without joy or zest, just to pass the time. Then Aesop, who was with me, sat up to listen, and I stop humming and listen too. There are voices outside, some people are coming. A chance thing, nothing out of the ordinary! A party of two men and a girl came bursting into the place. They shouted to one another, laughing, "Quick! We can take shelter here awhile."

I got up.

One of the men was wearing a white unstarched shirt front that was now baggy to boot, having been soaked by the rain; to this wet shirt front was pinned a diamond clip. On his feet he had long pointed shoes that looked somewhat foppish. I bowed to the man, it was Mr. Mack, the trader; I recognized him from the store where I'd bought bread. He had even invited me to call on him at home sometime, but I hadn't been there yet.

"Ah, we've met before!" he said, when he noticed me. "We were on our way out to the mill, but had to turn back. Some weather, eh? But when are you coming to Sirilund, Lieutenant?" He introduced the little black-bearded man who was with him, a doctor living near the chapel-of-ease.

The girl raised her veil a bit, up on her nose, and started talking to Aesop in a low voice. I noticed her jacket and could tell by the lining and the buttonholes that it had been dyed. Mr. Mack introduced her also, she was his daughter, Edvarda.

Edvarda threw a glance at me through her veil and went on whispering to the dog, reading what it said on his collar: "So, your name is Aesop, is it? . . . Doctor, who was Aesop? All I can remember is that he wrote fables. Wasn't he a Phrygian? No, I don't know."

A child, a schoolgirl. I looked at her—she was tall but with no figure, around fifteen or sixteen, with long, dusky hands without gloves. Maybe she had looked up "Aesop" in an encyclopedia that very afternoon, to have a ready answer.

Mr. Mack questioned me about my hunting. What did I shoot mostly? I could have one of his boats at my disposal whenever I liked, I just had to let him know. The Doctor didn't say a word. When the party left I noticed that the Doctor had a limp and used a stick.

I walked home in the same vacant mood as before, humming nonchalantly. This meeting in the boathouse hadn't affected me one way or the other; what I remembered best of it all was Mr. Mack's soaked shirt front with the diamond clip, that too wet and without much brilliance.

III

There was a rock in front of my hut, a tall, gray rock. By its looks it seemed to be well-disposed toward me, it was as if it saw me when I came by, and recognized me. I used to like walking past that rock when I went out in the morning, I felt as though I was leaving a good friend there, who would be waiting for me till I came back.

And up in the forest began the hunt. I might shoot something, or I might not.

Beyond the islands lay the sea in a leaden repose. I would watch it many a time from the hills, when I was high up; on calm days the ships barely moved, I would see the same sail for three days, small and white, like a gull on the water. But if the wind veered about, the mountains in the distance would almost disappear, we were in for rough weather, a southwester, a drama to which I was a spectator. Spindrift veiled the horizon,[2] earth and sky were confounded, the sea tossed in tortuous dances, forming men, horses and slashed banners in the air. I stood in the lee of a cliff thinking of all sorts of things, my soul was excited. God knows, I thought, what I'm witnessing today and why the sea opens[3] before my eyes! Maybe at this moment I behold the interior of the earth's brain, how it labors, everything seething! Aesop was restless, cocking his nose in the air and sniffing time and again, weather-sick, his legs quivering skittishly. But as I didn't speak to him, he lay down between my feet and gazed out to sea just like me. And not a cry, no human voice to be heard anywhere, nothing but that dull roar around my head. Far out lay a reef, alone; when the waves crashed against that reef, they reared up like a crazy spiral, or rather like a sea-god rising, wet, into the air to survey the world, blowing snorts that made his hair and beard stand out from his head like the spokes of a wheel. Then he plunged down into the surf again.

And in the midst of the storm a little coal-black steamer was fighting its way in from the sea. . . .

When I went down to the dock in the afternoon, the little coal-black steamer had entered the harbor; it was the packet boat. There were many people on the jetty, come to take a look at the rare visitor; I noticed that they all, without exception, had blue eyes, however different they might be otherwise. A young girl with a white woolen kerchief around her head stood some way off; she had very dark hair, and the white kerchief formed a strange contrast to her hair. She looked inquisitively at me, at my leather clothes and my gun; when I spoke to her she became embarrassed and turned her head away. I said, "You should always wear that white kerchief, it suits you." Just then she was joined by a heavy-limbed man in an Icelandic sweater, he called her Eva. Evidently she was his daughter. I knew the heavy-limbed man, he was the smith, the local blacksmith. He had installed a fresh nipple in one of my guns a few days ago. . . .

And rain and wind did their work and melted away the snow. For some days a cold, unsettled atmosphere hovered over the earth, rotten branches snapped, and the crows gathered in flocks and squawked. But it didn't go on for long, the sun was near, one morning it rose behind the forest. A shaft of sweetness shoots through me from top to toe when the sun rises; I shoulder my gun in silent exultation.

IV

There was no lack of game at this time, I shot what I wanted— a hare, a black grouse, a ptarmigan—and when I happened to be down by the shore and came within range of some sea bird or other, I shot that too. They were good times, the days were getting longer and the air more limpid. I would fix myself up for a couple of days and head for the mountains, onto the peaks, I met reindeer Lapps who gave me cheese, small, rich cheeses with a relish of herbs. I went there more than once. On my way back home again, I always shot some bird or other and put it in my bag. I sat down and tied up Aesop. Miles below me I could see the sea; the mountainsides were wet and black from the water trickling down them, dripping and trickling to the same tiny old melody. Those little melodies far away in the mountains helped me pass many an hour as I sat there looking around. Here is this little endless tune trickling away in solitude, I thought, and nobody ever hears it and nobody thinks about it, but still it goes on trickling to itself, on and on! And I no longer felt that the mountain was quite deserted when I heard that trickle. Once in a while something happened: a thunderclap would shake the earth, a rock come loose and plunge down to the sea, leaving behind a trail of smoking dust; the next moment Aesop would turn his nose to the wind, showing surprise as he sniffed the smell of burning he couldn't understand. When the snow water had forced crevices in the rock, a shot or even a sharp cry was enough to tear a big block loose and send it crashing down. . . .

An hour might go by, maybe more, time passed so quickly. I unleashed Aesop, slung my bag over the other shoulder and set out for home. The day was waning. Down in the woods I invariably hit upon my old familiar path, a narrow ribbon of a path with the most curious turns. I followed each bend taking my time, there was no hurry, nobody was waiting for me at home; free as a lord, I wandered about in the peaceful forest at my own sweet pace. The birds were all silent, only the blackcock was calling far away; it was always calling.

Coming out of the forest, I saw two people ahead of me, two people out for a walk. I caught up with them—one was

Miss Edvarda, I knew her and said hello; with her was the Doctor. I had to show them my gun, they inspected my compass and my bag; I invited them to my hut and they promised to come some day.

Evening had fallen. I went home and lighted a fire, roasted a bird and had a meal. Tomorrow was another day. . . .

A hushed stillness all around. I lie there looking out of the window till well into the evening. A faery light hovered over field and forest at that hour, the sun had set and colored the horizon with a rich red light, motionless as oil. The sky was everywhere open and pure; gazing into that clear sea, I felt as if I lay face to face with the very bedrock of the world, my heart beating warmly against that naked bedrock and being at home there. God knows, I thought to myself, why the horizon decks itself out in violet and gold tonight, whether some celebration isn't taking place up there in the world, a celebration in grand style, with music from the stars and boating parties down broad streams. It looks that way! And I closed my eyes and went along on the boating party, and thought upon thought sailed through my brain. . . .

Thus passed more than one day.

I wandered about observing how the snow was turning into water and how the ice was breaking up. Many days I didn't even fire a shot; when there was already food enough in the hut, I just roamed about at my leisure and let the time pass. Wherever I turned, there was always just as much to see and hear, everything changed a little each day, even the osiers and junipers were waiting for the spring. One place I went to was the mill, which was still icebound; but the ground around it had been trampled for ages and bore witness that people had come there with sacks of grain on their backs, to have it ground. It was as though I walked among people; besides, there were many letters and dates carved on the walls.

Ah, well!

V

Shall I write more? No, no. Just a little to amuse myself, and because it helps pass the time to tell how spring came two years back and how the country looked. The earth and the sea began to emit a faint odor, the dead leaves rotting in the woods gave off a sweetish smell of hydrogen sulfide, and the magpies flew with twigs in their beaks, building nests. Another couple of days, and the brooks began to swell and foam, a few tortoise-shell butterflies were seen, and the fishermen returned from their fishing stations. The trader's two smacks came in with a full load of fish and anchored off the drying grounds; suddenly there was a hustle and bustle out on the largest of the islands, where the fish were to be dried on the rocks.[4] I could see it all from my window.

But no noise reached my hut, I was alone and remained so. Every now and then someone would pass by; I saw Eva, the blacksmith's daughter, she now had a few freckles on her nose.

"Where are you going?" I asked.

"To fetch firewood," she replied, softly. She had a rope in her hand to carry the wood, and she had her white kerchief on her head. I followed her with my eyes, but she didn't turn her head.

Then many days went by before I saw anyone again.

Spring pressed ahead and the forest grew lighter. It was great fun to watch the thrushes in the tree tops, gazing at the sun and screeching; sometimes I was already up by two in the morning to share in the joyous mood emanating from birds and beasts when the sun rose.

Spring must also have come to me, and at times my blood seemed to pound like footfalls. I sat in my hut thinking I should check my fishing rods and trolling lines, but I didn't lift a finger to do anything; an obscure, joyous restlessness came and went in my heart. Then, suddenly, Aesop jumped up and, standing there on stiff legs, gave a short yelp. Some people were coming to the hut, I could already hear Edvarda's voice at the door as I quickly took off my cap. She and the Doctor were coming to call on me, kindly and unpretentiously, as they had promised.

"Yes, he's home," I heard her say. And she came up and gave me her hand, in a perfectly girlish way. "We were here yesterday, too, but you weren't home," she explained.

She sat down on my bed, on top of the coverlet, and gave a look around the hut; the Doctor sat down beside me on the long bench. We talked, chattering on and on; among other things I told them what kinds of animals there were in the forest and what game I could no longer shoot because it was out of season. Right now the black grouse was out of season.

The Doctor didn't say much this time either; but when he caught sight of my powder horn, with a figurine of Pan on it, he began to explain the myth of Pan.

"But," said Edvarda suddenly, "what do you live on when all the game is out of season?"

"On fish," I replied. "Mostly on fish. There's always food to be had."

"But you could come and eat with us, you know," she said. "Last year it was an Englishman who had your hut, and he came and ate with us quite often."

Edvarda looked at me, and I looked at her. In that moment I felt something touch my heart, like a fleeting affectionate greeting. It was the spring and the clear day, I have thought about it since. Besides, I admired her arched eyebrows.

She said a few words about my place. I had covered the walls with various animal skins and bird's wings, the hut looked like a furry lair inside. It met with her approval. "Yes, it's a lair," she said.

I had nothing to offer the visitors that they might like; after

some thought I decided to roast a bird, just for the fun of it.
They could eat it hunters' fashion, with their fingers. It might
be rather amusing.

I roasted the bird.

Edvarda told us about the Englishman. He was an old man,
an oddball who talked aloud to himself. He was a Catholic,
and wherever he came and went he had a little prayer book
with black and red letters in his pocket.

"He was an Irishman, then, perhaps," the Doctor said.

"Was he an Irishman?"

"Yes, don't you think, since he was a Catholic?"

Edvarda blushed, she stammered and looked away: "Well,
yes, maybe he was an Irishman."

From now on she lost her vivacity. Feeling sorry for her and
wanting to smooth things over, I said, "No, of course you're
right in saying he was English. The Irish don't travel to
Norway."

We arranged to row out and have a look at the cod-drying
rocks some day.

After walking my visitors a little way, I went back and got
down to work on my fishing gear. My bag net had been hanging on a nail by the door and several meshes had been damaged
by rust. I sharpened some hooks, fastened them on, and
checked the seines. How difficult it was to get anything done
today! Irrelevant thoughts came and went in my head; it
seemed to me I had made a gaffe in letting Miss Edvarda sit
on the bed the whole time, instead of offering her a seat on
the bench. Suddenly I saw her dusky face and neck before me.
She had tied her pinafore rather low on her hips to have a long
waist, as was the fashion; the chaste, girlish look of her thumb
affected me tenderly,[5] and the one or two wrinkles on her
knuckle were full of kindness. She had a large mouth, her lips
were flaming red.

I got up, opened the door and listened. I could hear nothing,
nor did I have anything to listen for. I closed the door again;

Aesop came out from his corner and noticed my restlessness. It occurred to me that I could run after Miss Edvarda and ask her for a bit of silk thread to mend my net with; it wasn't just a whim, I could produce the net and show her the meshes spoiled by rust. I was already outside the door when I remembered that I had silk thread myself, in my fly-book, more than I needed, in fact. And disheartened, I went quietly back in, since I had silk thread myself.

A breath of something unfamiliar wafted toward me as I entered the hut, it seemed as if I were no longer alone there.[6]

VI

A man asked me whether I had quit hunting; he hadn't heard me fire a single shot up in the hills, though he had been fishing in the bay for two days. No, I hadn't been hunting, I was staying home in my hut until I ran out of food.

On the third day I did go hunting. The forest was getting green, there was a fragrance of earth and trees, and the green leaves of the chive were already sticking up through the ice-burned moss. My head was full of thoughts and I sat down more than once. For three days I hadn't seen a soul except one person, the fisherman I met yesterday. I thought to myself, Perhaps I'll run across someone tonight when I go home, at the edge of the forest where I met the Doctor and Miss Edvarda the last time. They might very well take another stroll there, maybe and maybe not. But why did I think of just those two? I shot a couple of ptarmigan and prepared one of them at once; then I tied up Aesop.

I lay on the dry ground as I ate. The world was quiet all around, only a gentle sighing of the wind and the sound of a bird here and there. I lay and watched the branches swaying softly in the breeze; the little wind was doing its part, carrying pollen from twig to twig and filling each innocent stigma. The whole forest was in ecstasy. A green caterpillar, an inchworm, walks along a branch end by end, walks incessantly, as if it cannot rest. It sees next to nothing, though it does have eyes; often it rears straight up, feeling about in the air for something to bear up against. It looks like a bit of green thread sewing a seam with slow stitches along the branch. By evening, perhaps, it will have reached the place where it's going.

Always quiet. I get up and walk, sit down and get up again. It's about four o'clock; when it's six I'll start going home and see whether I meet anyone. There are two more hours till then, and I'm already a bit restless and brush the heather and moss from my clothes. I know the places I'll pass, the trees and the rocks stand there as before in their solitude, the leaves rustle under my feet. The monotonous soughing and the familiar trees and rocks mean a lot to me, I'm filled with a mysterious gratitude; everything befriends me, intermingles with me, I love all things. I pick up a dry twig, hold it in my hand and look at it as I sit there having my own thoughts. The twig is nearly rotten, its poor bark affects me, pity stirring my heart. And when I get up to go, I do not throw the twig away but lay it down and stand there feeling fond of it. Finally, with moist eyes, I give it one last look before leaving it there.

It's five o'clock. The sun tells me the wrong time; having walked westward all day, I may have gotten ahead of my sun marks at the hut by half an hour. I'm quite aware of all this, but I still have another hour before six o'clock, so I get up again and take a short walk. An hour or so goes by in this way.

Below me I can see the creek and the little mill, which has been icebound during the winter, and I stop; the mill is running, its hum rouses me, I stop short then and there. "I'll be late!" I say aloud. A pang rips through me, I turn at once and head for home, knowing full well that I'll be late. I begin to walk faster, to run; Aesop understands that something is up, he strains at the leash and drags me along, whining and bustling. The dry leaves crackle around us. But when we reached the edge of the forest there was nobody there; no, everything was quiet, there was nobody there.

There's nobody here! I say to myself. Anyhow, I had half expected it, no great loss.

I didn't stand there for long but went on, drawn by all my thoughts, past my hut and down to Sirilund, with Aesop and my bag and gun, with all my gear.

Mr. Mack received me with the utmost friendliness and invited me for supper.

VII

I believe I can read a little in the souls of those around me; maybe it is not so. Oh, when I have a good day I feel as if I can peer deep into other people's souls, although I don't have a particularly good head on my shoulders. We sit in a room, some men and women and I, and I seem to see what is going on in the hearts of these people and what they think of me. I put something into every flashing glance of their eyes; occasionally the blood rushes to their cheeks so they turn red, at other times they pretend to be looking another way while still watching me out of the corner of their eyes. There I sit observing all this, and nobody suspects that I see through every soul. For several years I have thought I could read the souls of everybody. Maybe it is not so. . . .

I remained at Mr. Mack's house all evening. I could have left again at once, I wasn't eager to stay on. But hadn't I come precisely because all my thoughts had drawn me there? Could I, then, go my way at once? After supper we played whist and drank toddy, I had my back to the room and sat with my head bowed; behind me Edvarda was going in and out. The Doctor had gone home.

Mr. Mack showed me how his new lamps worked, the first kerosene lamps that had come north, showpieces on huge leaden feet; he lighted them every evening himself to forestall accidents. Once or twice he spoke about his grandfather, the consul: "My grandfather, Consul Mack, received this clip from King Carl Johan's own hands," he said, pointing his finger at the diamond clip. His wife had died, he showed me a painting of her in one of the side rooms, a genteel-looking woman with a lace cap and a polite smile. In the same room there was also a bookcase, which even had some old French books in it, ostensibly heirlooms. They had fine, gilded bindings, and many owners had inscribed their names in them. Among the books were several educational works; Mr. Mack was a thinking man.

His two store clerks had to be summoned for the whist; they played slowly and diffidently, counted over carefully and still made mistakes. One of them was helped by Edvarda.

Then I upset my glass; I felt miserable and stood up. "Oh —I've upset my glass!" I said.

Edvarda burst out laughing and replied, "Yes, that's plain enough."

They all assured me laughingly that it didn't matter. They gave me a towel to dry myself with and we went on playing. Soon it was eleven o'clock.

An obscure feeling of resentment shot through me at Edvarda's laughter, I looked at her and found that her face had become commonplace and quite plain. Finally Mr. Mack broke up the game on the pretext that his two clerks had to go to bed; then, leaning back in the sofa, he began to talk about putting up a sign on his warehouse front and asked my advice about it. What color should he use? I was bored and answered "black," without giving it any thought, and Mr. Mack at once said the same, "Black, just what I've been thinking myself. 'SALT AND BARRELS IN STOCK,' in big black letters, that's the most dignified. . . . Edvarda, shouldn't you be going to bed now?"

Edvarda got up, gave us both her hand for good night and left. We stayed on. We talked about the railroad that had been completed last year, and about the first telegraph line. God only knew when the telegraph would come up north! Pause.

"You see," Mr. Mack said, "step by step I've reached the age of forty-six, my hair and beard are gray. Yes, I do feel I'm getting on in years. Seeing me during the day, you may think I'm young, but when evening comes and I'm alone, I flag considerably. Then I just sit here in the parlor playing solitaire. It usually comes out with a bit of cheating. Ha-ha!"

"Your patience comes out with a bit of cheating?" I asked.

"Yes."

It seemed to me I could read his eyes. . . .

He got up, took a turn over to the window and looked out; he appeared very stoop-shouldered, and his neck and throat were furry. I also got up. Turning around, he came toward me in his long pointed shoes, keeping both thumbs in his vest pockets and flapping his arms a little, like wings, all the while smiling. Then once more he offered to put a boat at my disposal and gave me his hand.

"Come to think, let me go with you," he said and blew out the lamps. "Yes, I'll take a little walk, it's not late yet."

We went out.

He pointed up the road toward the blacksmith's house and said, "This way! It's the shortest."

"No," I replied, "it's shorter to go around by the docks."

We exchanged a few words about this without coming to an agreement. I was convinced that I was right and couldn't understand his insistence. Finally he suggested that we should go our separate ways; the one who got there first should wait at the hut.

We were off. He soon disappeared into the forest.

I walked at my usual pace and figured I would get there at

least five minutes ahead of him. But when I reached the hut he was already there. He called out to me as I came up, "There, you see! No, I always come this way, it really is shorter."

I looked at him in great surprise, he wasn't warm and didn't seem to have been running. He took his leave at once, thanked me for a pleasant evening and went back the same way he had come.

I stood there thinking, How odd! I should be a fairly good judge of distance, and I've gone both ways several times. My dear man, you're cheating again! Was it all a pretense?

I saw his back disappearing into the forest again.

The next moment I was following him, quickly and warily; I could see him wiping his face all along, and I was no longer sure that he hadn't been running. He was now walking very slowly and I kept an eye on him; he stopped at the blacksmith's house. I took cover and saw the door being opened and Mr. Mack entering the house.

It was one o'clock, I could tell by the sea and by the grass.

VIII

A few days went by as best they could, my only friend was the forest and the great solitude. Good God, never before had I been more alone than on the first of those days. Spring was in full tilt; I found starflowers and yarrow in the fields, and both the chaffinches and the bramblings had arrived, I knew all the birds. Sometimes I would take two quarters from my pocket and chink them together to break the solitude. I thought, What if Diderik and Iselin came along!

It was beginning to be no night, the sun barely dipped its disk into the sea before it rose again, red, renewed, as if it had been down to drink. What strange adventures I met with at

night sometimes; nobody would believe it. Wasn't Pan sitting
in a tree watching to see how I would comport myself? Wasn't
his belly open, and wasn't he hunched over so that he seemed
to be drinking from his own belly? But all this he did only so
he could cock his eye and watch me, and the whole tree shook
from his silent laughter when he saw that my thoughts were
running away with me. There was a rustling all over the forest.
Animals snuffled, birds called one another, their signals filled
the air. It was a year when the cockchafers were particularly
numerous; their buzzing mingled with that of the moths, it
sounded like whisperings through the forest, back and forth.
How much there was to listen to! I went without sleep for
three nights, thinking of Diderik and Iselin.

Look, I thought, they might come. And Iselin would lure
Diderik up to a tree and say, Stay here, Diderik, and watch,
keep guard over Iselin, I'll let this hunter tie my shoelace.

The hunter, that's me, and she will give me a sign with her
eyes to make me understand. And when she comes my heart
understands all, and it no longer beats, it peals. And she is naked
under her dress[7] from head to foot, and I lay my hand upon
her.

Tie my shoelace! she says with flaming cheeks. And a little
later she whispers directly against my mouth, against my lips,
Oh, you're not tying my shoelace, sweetheart, you're not tying . . . not tying my . . .

But the sun dips its disk into the sea and then rises again,
red, renewed, as if it has been down to drink. And the air is
full of whisperings.

An hour later she says against my mouth, Now I must leave
you.

And she waves back to me as she goes, her cheeks still flaming; her face is tender and rapturous. And again she turns and
waves to me.

But Diderik steps forward from the tree and says, Iselin, what
were you doing? I saw you.

She answers, Diderik, what did you see? I did nothing.

Iselin, I saw you do it, he says again. I saw it.[8]

Then her loud, merry laughter rings through the forest and she goes off with him, exultant and sinful from top to toe. And where does she go? To her next lover, a hunter in the forest.[9]

It was midnight. Aesop had broken loose and was hunting on his own, I could hear him baying up in the hills, and when I finally brought him back it was one o'clock. A shepherd girl came along, she was knitting a stocking and humming while looking about her. But where was her flock? And what was she walking around for in the forest at midnight? Oh, for nothing, nothing. For restlessness, or for happiness perhaps, no matter. I thought, She heard Aesop barking and knew I was in the forest.

I had stood up and was looking at her as she came, and I saw how young and thin she was. Aesop also stood and looked at her.

"Where are you coming from?" I asked her.

"From the mill," she replied.

But what could she have been doing at the mill so late at night?

"How come you're not afraid to walk in the forest so late at night," I said, "young and thin as you are?"

She laughed and replied, "I'm not that young, I'm nineteen."

But she couldn't be nineteen, I'm convinced she was lying by two years and was only seventeen. But why did she lie and make herself older?

"Sit down," I said, "and tell me your name."

And blushing, she sat down beside me and said her name was Henriette.

I asked, "Do you have a sweetheart, Henriette, and has he ever held you in his arms?"

"Yes," she answered, laughing shyly.

"How many times already?"

She's silent.

"How many times?" I repeat.

"Twice," she said softly.

I drew her toward me and asked, "How did he do it? Did he do it like this?"

"Yes," she whispered, trembling.

Then it was four o'clock.[10]

IX

I had a conversation with Edvarda. "It's going to rain soon," I said.

"What time is it?" she asked.

I looked at the sun and replied, "Around five."

She asked, "Can you tell it that exactly by the sun?"

"Yes," I replied, "I can."

Pause.

"But what if you can't see the sun, how do you know the time then?"

"Then I go by other things. There is high tide and low tide, there's the grass that settles at a certain hour, and the changing birdcalls; some birds begin to sing when others are silent. And I can tell the time by the flowers that close in the afternoon, and by the leaves, which now are bright green, now dark green. Besides, I have a hunch."

"I see," she said.

I was expecting rain, and loath, for Edvarda's sake, to detain her any longer in the middle of the road, I touched my cap. But then, suddenly, she stopped me with a fresh question and I stayed. She blushed and asked me what I was really doing up here, why I went hunting, why this, that and the other. After all, I shot only what was strictly necessary, for food, letting Aesop remain idle?[11]

She blushed and looked humble. I understood that someone had been talking about me and that she had overheard it, she was not speaking for herself. My feelings were touched, she looked so forlorn—it struck me that she was motherless, her thin arms gave her a neglected appearance. It just came over me.

Well, I didn't shoot to murder, I shot in order to live. I needed *one* grouse today and so I didn't shoot two, I'd shoot the other one tomorrow. Why should I shoot more? I lived in the forest, I was a son of the forest. Anyway, from the first of June ptarmigan and hare were out of season, so I would have practically nothing to shoot anymore; well and good, I would go fishing and live on fish. I would get a boat from her father for rowing out in. No, I was not a hunter just so I could shoot things, of course not, but to be able to live in the forest. I felt comfortable there; I could lie at table, on the ground, when I ate, I didn't have to sit straight up and down on a chair; and I did not upset my glass. In the forest I forbade myself nothing, I could lie on my back and close my eyes if I wished, I could also say anything I liked there. Often when you had something you wanted to say and you said it out loud, it sounded like a voice from the very heart of the forest. . . .

When I asked her if she understood that, she answered "Yes."

I went on to say more, because her eyes lingered on me. "If you just knew all the things I see out in the wild," I said. "In the winter, walking along, I may see ptarmigan tracks in the snow. Suddenly the tracks disappear, the birds have flown up. But I can tell from the imprint of the wings in what direction the game has flown, and before long I hunt it up. Each time it's a bit different. Many a time in the fall you may chance to see shooting stars. What was that? I then think to myself in my solitude. A world seized by convulsions, a world breaking up before my very eyes? To think that I—that *I* was privileged to see a shooting star in my life! And when the summer comes, there may be a tiny living creature on every leaf; I can see that some have no wings, they can't get anywhere—they must live and die on the little leaf where they came into the world. Just imagine! Sometimes I see a bluebottle. Well, all this doesn't sound like very much, I don't know if you understand."

"Yes, yes, I understand."

"Well. And then sometimes I look at the grass, and maybe the grass looks back at me, what do we know? I look at a single blade of grass, perhaps it's trembling a little—that is already something, it seems to me. I think to myself, Look, this blade of grass is trembling! And if it is a pine tree I'm looking at, then perhaps it has a branch which makes me cherish that too a little. But sometimes I also meet people up in the hills, yes, it happens."

I looked at her—she was listening, craning her neck forward. I couldn't recognize her. She was so attentive that she dropped her guard, became ugly and stupid-looking, her lower lip sagging badly.

"Really!" she said, straightening up.

The first raindrops fell.

"It's raining," I said.

"Yes, just think, it's raining," she said too, and was gone.

I didn't walk her home, she went off by herself while I hurried up to my hut. A few minutes passed, it began to rain heavily. Suddenly I hear someone come running after me, I stop and see Edvarda. She had turned red from the exertion and smiled.

"I forgot," she said breathlessly. "About that outing to the drying grounds, the cod-drying rocks.[12] The Doctor is coming tomorrow, do you have time then?"

"Tomorrow? All right. Sure, I have time."

"I forgot," she said again and smiled.

As she left I noticed her beautiful slender legs, they were wet high up. Her shoes were worn down.

X

I can still remember one day very well. It was the day when my summer came. The sun began shining when it was still night and had dried the wet ground by morning, the air had become nice and soft after the latest rain.

I showed up on the pier in the afternoon. The water was perfectly still, we could hear laughter and talking coming from the island where the men and girls were busy with the fish. It was a happy afternoon.

Yes, wasn't it a happy afternoon? We had baskets of food and wine with us, a large party of people divided between two boats, with young women in light-colored dresses. I was so delighted, I hummed to myself.

Once in the boat I wondered where all those young people had come from. There were the daughters of the Sheriff and the district doctor, a couple of governesses, and the ladies from the parsonage; I had never seen them before, they were strangers to me and yet so trusting, as if we'd known one another a long time. I committed a few gaffes. I was no longer accustomed to mixing with people and often addressed the young ladies by their first names; but they didn't mind. Once I said "Dear" or "My dear," but they pardoned me for that as well and pretended that I hadn't said it.

Mr. Mack had his unstarched shirt front on as usual, with the diamond clip. He seemed to be in excellent spirits and called over to the other boat, "Take good care of the baskets with the bottles, you crazy people! Doctor, you'll answer for the bottles!"

"All right!" the Doctor answered back. And coming over the water from one boat to another, those two calls alone sounded festive and jolly in my ears.

Edvarda was wearing her dress from yesterday, as if she didn't have any other dress or refused to put it on. Her shoes were also the same. Her hands weren't quite clean, it seemed to me; but she had a brand-new hat on her head, with a feather in it. She had brought her dyed jacket to sit on.

At Mr. Mack's request I fired a shot as we were about to land—two shots, both barrels, followed by shouts of hurrah. We walked up on the island; the dryers greeted us all, and Mr. Mack talked to his workers. We found daisies and butter-cups, which we put in our buttonholes; some of us found bluebells.

And masses of sea birds quacked and cried in the air and on the shore.

We camped on a grassy plot with a few stunted white birches, the baskets were uncovered and Mr. Mack uncorked the bottles. Light dresses, blue eyes, the tinkling of glasses, the sea, the white sails. We sang snatches of song.

And our cheeks became rosy.[13]

An hour later my thoughts are sheer exultation. Even little things touch me: a veil flutters on a hat, someone's hair is let down, a pair of eyes close with laughter and I am moved. What a day, what a day!

"I hear you have such an amusing little hut, Lieutenant."

"Yes, a nest. God, all my heart could desire! Come and see me some day, miss; it's one of a kind. And behind the hut there's a large forest."

Another girl comes up and says amicably, "You haven't been up north before, have you?"

"No," I reply. "But already I know all about it, my good ladies. At night I'm face to face with the mountains, the earth and the sun. But I won't try to be pompous. What a summer you have up here! It springs forth some night when everyone is asleep, and in the morning there it is. I looked out of my window and saw it myself. I have two small windows."

A third one comes up. I find her charming because of her voice and her small hands. How charming they all are! The third one says, "Shall we exchange flowers? It brings good luck."

"Sure," I said, holding out my hand, "let's exchange flowers, thank you for that. How pretty you are! You have a charming voice, I've been hearing it all the time."

But she withdraws her bluebells and says curtly, "What's the matter with you? I didn't mean you."

She hadn't meant me! It grieved me that I'd made a mistake, I wished I were home again, far away in my hut where only the wind spoke to me. "I'm sorry," I say, "forgive me." The other ladies look at one another and go away so as not to humiliate me.

At this moment someone came quickly toward us, everyone saw her, it was Edvarda. She comes straight up to me, says a few words and falls on my neck—she clasps her arms around my neck and kisses me on the lips again and again. She says something each time, but I can't hear what it is. I couldn't understand the whole thing, my heart had stopped, I just noticed the burning look in her eyes. When she let go of me, her little bosom rose and fell. There she stood, lingering, with her dusky face and neck, tall and slim, with flashing eyes, completely reckless; everyone was staring at her. For the second time I was thrilled by her dark eyebrows, which rose in a high curve on her forehead.

But good God, the girl had kissed me in front of everybody!

"What is it, Miss Edvarda?" I asked, and I hear my blood throbbing, hear it as it were from my throat, it prevents me from speaking clearly.

"Oh, nothing," she answers. "I just felt like it. It doesn't matter."

I take off my cap and mechanically brush my hair back as I stand looking at her. Doesn't it matter? I thought.

Then Mr. Mack's voice is heard from another part of the island, saying something that we cannot hear. I'm glad to think that Mr. Mack has seen nothing, knows nothing. How lucky that he was in another part of the island just now! This makes me feel relieved, I step up to the rest of the company and say laughingly, acting very nonchalant, "May I beg you all to pardon my unseemly behavior a while ago; I feel terribly upset about it. I took advantage of a moment when Miss Edvarda wished to exchange flowers with me to offend her; I apologize to her and to you all. Put yourselves in my place: I live alone, I'm not used to associating with ladies; besides, I've been drinking wine today, which I'm not used to either. Please, bear with me."

I laughed, acting nonchalant about the whole trifling business to consign it to oblivion; but in my heart I was serious. Anyhow, my words were lost on Edvarda, who didn't attempt to hide anything or to erase the impression of her rashness; on the contrary, she sat down close to me and kept looking at me the whole time. Every now and then she would say something to me. Later on, when we were playing "widower," she said loudly, "Lieutenant Glahn is the one I want. I don't feel like running after anyone else."

"Damn it all, woman, why don't you pipe down!" I whispered, stamping my foot.

A look of surprise flitted across her face, she made a pained grimace with her nose and smiled shyly. I was deeply moved, unable to resist that forlorn expression of her eyes and of her whole thin figure. I fell in love with her and took her long, narrow hand in mine.

"Later!" I said. "No more now. We can meet tomorrow, you know."

XI

During the night I heard Aesop get up from his corner and growl, I could hear it in my sleep; but as I was having a dream about hunting just then, his growl blended into my dream and I didn't quite wake up from it. When I stepped out of the hut around two in the morning, there were tracks in the grass from a pair of feet; somebody had been there, had gone first up to one of my windows, then to the other. The footprints disappeared again down the road.

She came toward me with flaming cheeks, her face absolutely beaming.

"Have you been waiting?" she said. "I was afraid you might have to wait."

I had not been waiting, she had got a start on me.

"Did you sleep well?" I said. I couldn't think of anything much to say.

"No, I didn't, I've been awake," she replied. And she told me she hadn't slept all night, but had sat in a chair with her eyes closed. She had also been out for a while.

"Someone was outside my hut last night," I said. "I saw footprints in the grass this morning."

Her face turns crimson, she takes my hand there on the road and doesn't answer. I look at her and ask, "Was it you, perhaps?"

"Yes," she replied, pressing herself up against me, "it was me. I didn't wake you up, did I? I stepped as quietly as I could. Oh yes, it was me. I was near you once more. I love you."

XII

I met her every day, every day. I honestly admit I was glad to
see her, my heart had taken wing. It's two years ago this summer; now I think of it only when I feel like it, the whole
adventure amuses and distracts me. And as far as the two green
feathers are concerned, I'll explain it shortly.

There were several places where we met, at the mill, on the
road, even in my hut; she came wherever I wanted her to.
"Hi!" she called, always before I did, and I answered "Hi."

"You're happy today, you're singing," she says, her eyes
sparkling.

"Yes, I'm happy," I answer. "You have a spot there, on
your shoulder, it's dust, a piece of dirt from the road perhaps.
I want to kiss that spot, yes, please, let me kiss it! Everything
about you affects me so tenderly, I'm crazy about you. I didn't
sleep last night."

And it was true, I lay sleepless more than one night.

We stroll down the road side by side.

"What do you think, am I behaving as you like me to?" she
says. "Maybe I talk too much? No? Oh, but you must tell me
what you think. Sometimes I tell myself that this will never
end well. . . ."

"What will never end well?" I ask.

"This thing with us. That it won't end well. Believe me or
not, but I'm freezing right now; I get shivers down my spine
the moment I come near you. From happiness."

"Yes, me too," I answer, "I too get the shivers, just from
seeing you. Sure, it will be all right. Anyway, I'll pat your back
a bit and warm you."

Grudgingly, she lets me do it. I pat her a little harder, just
for fun, laughing and asking if it helps any.

"Oh, no. Please, don't be so kind as to thump my back anymore," she says.

Those few words! It sounded so helpless to me, the way she said, "Please, don't be so kind."

Then we walked on down the road. Is she annoyed with me because of my joke? I asked myself and thought, Let's see. I said, "I just remembered something. Once on a sleigh ride a young lady took a white silk scarf from her own neck and tied it around mine. In the evening I said to the lady, 'I'll return your scarf to you tomorrow, I'll have it washed.' 'No,' she answers, 'let me have it now, I want to keep it as it is, just as you have worn it.' And I gave her the scarf. Three years later I met the young lady again. 'The scarf?' I said. She brought the scarf. It lay in its wrapping, as unwashed as ever, I saw it myself."

Edvarda glanced up at me. "Well? What happened then?"

"Nothing, that's all," I said. "But I do think it was a nice touch."

Pause.

"Where is that lady now?"

"Abroad."

We spoke no more about it. But when she was about to go home she said, "Good night, then. Don't think about that lady anymore, will you? I think about no one but you."

I believed her. I saw that she meant what she said, and as long as she thought about me it was more than good enough. I went after her.

"Thanks, Edvarda!" I said. And then I added with all my heart, "You're much too good for me, but I'm grateful that you will have me; God will reward you for it. I may not be as grand as many others you could have, but I'm so utterly yours, so fervently yours, by my immortal soul. What are you thinking of? You have tears in your eyes."

"It's nothing," she answered. "It sounded so wonderful that

God would reward me for it. You say things that . . . Oh, I love you so!"

Suddenly she flung herself around my neck, right in the middle of the road, and kissed me ardently.

When she had gone, I turned aside and slipped into the forest, to hide and be alone with my happiness. And all stirred up, I ran back to the road again to see whether anyone might have noticed that I'd gone in there. But I saw no one.

XIII

Summer nights and still waters and endlessly still forests. Not a cry, not a footfall on the roads; my heart was full, as of dark wine.

Sphinx moths and other moths come flying soundlessly in through my window, lured by the light of the fireplace and by the smell of my roasted bird. They bump against the ceiling with a dull sound, buzz past my ears sending cold shivers through me, and settle on my white powder horn on the wall. I watch them, they sit there trembling and look at me—silk moths, goat moths and common moths. Some of them look to me like flying pansies.

I step outside the hut and listen. Nothing, not a sound, everything is asleep. The air sparkles with flying insects, myriads of buzzing wings. Over by the edge of the forest there are ferns and wolfsbane; the bearberry is in bloom and I love its tiny flowers. I thank you, God, for every ling flower I've ever seen; they've been like little roses on my path and I weep for love of them. Someplace nearby there are maiden pinks, I don't see them but I can scent their perfume.

But now, in the night hours, large white flowers have suddenly unfolded in the forest, their stigmas are open, they are breathing. And furry twilight moths dip down into their petals, setting the whole plant trembling. I go from one flower to another, they are in ecstasy; the flowers are steeped in an erotic[14] ecstasy, and I can see them falling into ecstasy.[15]

Light footsteps, someone's breath, a happy "Good evening."

I answer, throw myself down on the road and embrace her knees and her poor dress.

"Good evening, Edvarda!" I say again, faint with happiness.

"How you must love me!" she whispers.

"How grateful I must be!" I reply. "You're mine, and my heart lies still inside me all day long, thinking of you. You are the loveliest girl on earth, and I have kissed you. Often I turn red with joy simply by remembering I've kissed you."

"Why have you fallen so in love with me just tonight?" she asks.

There was no end to the reasons why, I had needed only to think of her to feel that way. That look from under the arched eyebrows, high up on her forehead, and that lovely dark skin!

"How could I not be in love with you?" I say. "I go around thanking each tree that you're well and in good health. Once at a ball there was a young lady who sat out dance after dance, and everyone let her just sit there. I didn't know her, but her face made an impression on me and I invited her to dance. 'Well?' No, she shook her head. 'You don't dance?' I said. 'Can you imagine,' she said, 'my father was so handsome and my mother was a perfect beauty, and my father swept my mother off her feet. But I was born lame'."

Edvarda looked at me. "Let's sit down," she said.

We sat down in the heather.

"Do you know what my friend says about you?" she began. "You have animal eyes, she says, and when you look at her it makes her go wild. It's as if you touched her, she says."

A strange joy fluttered through me when I heard this, not for my own sake but for Edvarda's, and I thought, There's only

one that I care about, what does she say about the look in my
eyes? I asked, "What friend was that?"

"That I won't tell you," she replied. "But it was one of
those who went with us to the drying grounds."

"I see," I said.

Then we talked about other things.

"My father is going to Russia in a few days," she said, "and
then I'll throw a party. Have you been out to Korholmerne?
We'll have two basketfuls of wine, the ladies from the parsonage will join the party again, my father has already given me
the wine. And you mustn't look at my friend again, promise?
You won't, will you? Or she'll not be invited."

And without another word she flung her arms around my
neck and looked at me, gazing into my face and breathing
audibly. Her eyes were quite black.

I stood up abruptly and just said, in my confusion, "So your
father is going to Russia?"

"Why did you get up so quickly?" she asked.

"Because it's late, Edvarda," I said. "Now the white flowers
are closing again, the sun is rising, it'll soon be day."

I walked her through the forest and kept following her with
my eyes as long as I could; way down, she turned around and
called a muffled good night. Then she was gone. At the same
moment the blacksmith's door opened, a man with a white
shirt front came out, looked about him, pulled his hat further
over his eyes and headed down toward Sirilund.

Edvarda's good night was still ringing in my ears.

XIV

Gladness is intoxicating. I fire my gun and an unforgettable
echo answers from crag to crag, floats out over the sea and

rings in some sleepless helmsman's ears. What am I glad about? A thought that comes to me, a memory, a sound in the forest, a human being. I think of her—I close my eyes and stand still on the road and think of her, counting the minutes.

Now I'm thirsty and drink from the brook; now I count a hundred paces one way and a hundred paces back; now it's late, I think to myself.

Is something the matter? A month has gone by, and a month is not a long time; there's nothing the matter! God knows, this month has been short. But the nights are often long, and I take it into my head to dip my cap in the brook and let it dry again, just to pass the time while I wait.

I reckoned my time in nights. Occasionally there would be a night when Edvarda stayed away; once she stayed away for two nights. Two nights! There was nothing the matter, but still I felt that perhaps my happiness had reached its peak.

And hadn't it?

"Do you hear, Edvarda, how restless it is in the forest to-night? There's a ceaseless rustling in the undergrowth, and the big leaves are trembling. Perhaps something is brewing; but that's not what I wanted to say. I hear a bird singing up in the hills; it's only a tit, but it has been sitting in the same place for two nights, calling. Can you hear it, that one monotonous sound?"

"Yes, I can hear it. Why do you ask me that?"

"For nothing. It has been sitting there for two nights. I just wanted to tell you. . . . Thanks, thanks for coming tonight, my love! I sat here waiting for you to come, tonight or to-morrow night, looking forward to it when you came."

"And I too have been waiting. I keep thinking of you, and I've collected the broken pieces of the glass you upset once and put them away; do you remember? My father left last night, I had a valid excuse for not coming, with so much to pack and to remind him of. I knew you were waiting here in the woods, and I cried and packed."

But two nights have gone by, I thought, what was she doing the first night? And why isn't there as much joy in her eyes as before?

An hour went by. The tit up in the hills had stopped singing, the forest was dead. No, no, there was nothing the matter, everything was as before, she gave me her hand for good night and looked lovingly at me.

"Tomorrow?" I said.

"No, not tomorrow," she replied.

I didn't ask why.

"Tomorrow, you know, we'll be having our party," she said, laughing. "I just wanted to surprise you, but you looked so miserable, I had to tell you right away. I was going to send you a written invitation."

My heart felt immensely relieved.

She left, nodding for goodbye.

"One more thing," I said, without moving. "How long has it been since you gathered up those pieces of broken glass and put them away?"

"How long it has been since then?"

"Yes, can it have been a week ago, two weeks ago?"

"Well, it may have been two weeks ago. But why do you ask about that? No, I'll tell you the truth: I did it yesterday."

She did it yesterday, she'd been thinking of me no longer ago than yesterday! Now all was well.

XV

The two boats lay on the water and we went on board. We sang and we talked. Korholmerne lay out beyond the islands, it took quite a while to row there, and in the meantime we talked to one another from the boats. The Doctor was tricked out in bright-colored clothes, as were the ladies; I'd never seen him so cheerful before, he joined in the conversation and was no longer a silent listener. I got the impression that he had been drinking a little and felt happy. When we landed, he requested the attention of the party for a moment and wished us welcome. I thought to myself, Why, Edvarda has chosen him to be host!

He entertained the ladies in a most amiable manner. Toward Edvarda he was courteous and kind, often fatherly and, as so many times before, inclined to give her pedantic lectures. Referring to a date, she said at one point, "I was born in thirty-eight," and he asked, "Eighteen hundred and thirty-eight, I suppose you mean?" If she then had answered, No, in nineteen hundred and thirty-eight, he would have shown no bewilderment but simply corrected her again and said, That surely must be wrong.[16] When I said something, he listened politely and attentively and didn't overlook me.

A young girl came up and said hello to me. Not being able to recognize or remember her, I uttered a few words of surprise, which made her laugh. It was one of the Dean's daughters, I had met her on the drying grounds and had invited her to my hut. We talked for a while.

An hour or two go by. I'm bored, drink the wine they pour out for me, mingle with everybody and chat with all. Again I commit a few gaffes, I'm on slippery ground and don't know right off how to respond to a kindness. Sometimes I ramble on or else become tongue-tied, and I fret over it. Over by the big rock we are using as a table, the Doctor sits gesticulating.

Soul! What sort of a thing was the soul? he was saying. The Dean's daughter had accused him of being a freethinker. Well, shouldn't you think freely? People imagined hell as a place underground with the devil as manager—or even a royal highness. He held forth about the altarpiece in the chapel-of-ease:

a Christ, a few Jews and Jewesses, water into wine—well and good! But Christ had a halo around his head. And what was a halo? A yellow hoop perched on three hairs.

Two of the ladies clapped their hands in horror. But the Doctor got out of the difficulty, saying playfully, "It does sound frightful, doesn't it? I admit that. But if you repeat it and repeat it to yourself seven or eight times and give a little thought to it, then it will sound better already. . . . And now, ladies, may I have the honor of drinking a glass with you?"

And he kneeled down on the grass in front of the two ladies, without removing his hat and putting it down before him, but holding it aloft with his left hand as he emptied the glass, his head thrown back. I was quite carried away by his great self-confidence and would have taken a glass with him myself if he hadn't already emptied his.

Edvarda was following him with her eyes. I took my stand near her and said, "Are we going to play 'widower' today?"

She gave a little start and got up. "Don't forget, we're not on a first-name basis now," she whispered.

In fact, I hadn't addressed her familiarly. I walked away again.

Another hour goes by. The day dragged on, I would have rowed home by myself long ago if there had been a third boat; Aesop lay tied up in the hut, maybe he was thinking of me. Edvarda's thoughts were certainly far removed from me, she was talking about the blessing of being able to go away, to other places; it made her cheeks glow and she even misspoke, "Nobody would be more happier than I the day—"

"More happier?" the Doctor says.

"What?" she asks.

"More happier."

"I don't understand."

"You said 'more happier,' that's all."

"I did? Sorry. Nobody would be happier than I the day I

found myself on board ship. Sometimes I long for places I don't even know of."

She longed to be away, she didn't remember me. I stood there watching her face and could tell she had forgotten me. Well, she couldn't be blamed for that; but I could read it clearly in her face. And the minutes crawled by, dismally slow. I asked several people whether we shouldn't row back now; it was getting late, I said, and Aesop lay tied up in the hut. But nobody wanted to go back.

I walked over to the Dean's daughter a third time, thinking, She must be the one who has talked about my animal eyes. We drank a glass together; she had trembling eyes, they were never at rest, she kept eyeing me continually and then looked away again.[17]

"Tell me, miss," I said, "don't you think that the people in these parts are very much like their short summer? That they are just as fickle and as charming?"

I spoke loudly, very loudly, and I did so on purpose. I continued to speak in a loud voice and asked the young lady once more to come visit me and see my hut. "God will bless you for it," I said in my distress, and I was already thinking to myself that I could find some present for her if she came. It might be, though, that my powder horn was the only thing I had, I thought.

And the young lady promised to come.

Edvarda sat with her face turned away and let me talk to my heart's content. She listened to all else being said and put in a word herself now and then. The Doctor read the palms of the young ladies and jabbered away; he himself had small delicate hands, with a ring on one finger. I felt unwanted and sat down by myself on a stone for a while. The afternoon was wearing on. Here I sit all alone on a stone, I said to myself, and the only person who could get me away from here lets me sit. Anyway, I don't really care.

A feeling of utter desolation took possession of me. My ears were ringing with the conversation behind me, and I could hear Edvarda laughing. At that laughter I suddenly got up and walked over to the company. My agitation was running away with me.

"Just a moment," I said. "It occurred to me while sitting over there that you might like to see my fly-book." And I took out my fly-book. "I'm sorry I didn't think of it before. Won't you, please, look through it, it would give me great pleasure; you must see it all, there are both red and yellow flies in it." I was holding my cap in my hand as I spoke. Then I became aware I had taken off my cap and that this was wrong, so I put it on again at once.

There was a moment of deep silence and nobody took the book. Finally the Doctor held out his hand for it and said politely, "Thank you, let's have a look at the things. It has always been a mystery to me how flies are put together."

"I make them myself," I said, full of gratitude toward him. And I began at once to explain how I made them. It was so simple, I bought the feathers and the hooks—they weren't very well made, of course, but then they were only for my own use. One could get ready-made flies, and they were very beautiful.

Edvarda threw an indifferent glance at me and my book and went on talking with her lady friends.

"Here are some materials too," the Doctor said. "Look, what lovely feathers."

Edvarda looked up.

"The green ones are pretty," she said. "Let me see them, Doctor."

"Keep them," I cried. "Yes, please, do me that favor today. They are two green bird's feathers. Do me a kindness, let it be a remembrance."[18]

She looked at them and said, "They are green or gold depending on how one holds them in the sun. Well, thanks, since you want to give them to me."

"Yes, I do want to give them to you," I said.

She took the feathers.

Shortly afterward the Doctor handed the book back to me and thanked me. Then he got up and asked if we shouldn't start thinking of getting back pretty soon.

I said, "Yes, for God's sake! I have a dog lying at home. You see, I have a dog, he's my friend; he lies there thinking of me, and when I come home he stands with his paws in the window to greet me. It has been such a lovely day, it's nearly over, let's row back. I thank you all."

I waited on the beach to see which boat Edvarda would choose and decided to take the other one. Suddenly she called me. I looked at her in surprise, her face was flushed. Then she came up to me, gave me her hand and said tenderly, "Thanks for the feathers. . . . Come, we're going in the same boat, aren't we?"

"If you want to," I replied.

We got into the boat; she took a seat beside me, on my thwart, I could feel her knee. I looked at her, and she returned my look for a moment. It did me good to have her touching me with her knee, and I was beginning to feel rewarded for that bitter day and to regain my joyful mood again, when she suddenly changed her position, turned her back on me and started talking to the Doctor, who sat at the tiller. For a full quarter of an hour I didn't exist for her. Then I did something I regret and haven't yet forgotten. Her shoe slipped off her foot, and I grabbed it and flung it far out over the water— whether for joy at her being so near or from some urge to assert myself and remind her of my existence, I don't know. It all happened so quickly, I didn't think, I just had that impulse. The ladies raised an outcry. I myself felt as though paralyzed by what I had done, but what was the use of that? It was done. The Doctor came to my aid, crying, "Row away!" and steered for the shoe. And the next moment the oarsman had caught it, just as it filled with water and[19] was sinking below the sur-

face; the man got his arm thoroughly wet. Then there was a
chorus of hurrahs from both boats because the shoe had been
saved.

I was deeply ashamed, and I felt my face change color and
screw itself up as I dried the shoe with my handkerchief. Edvarda accepted it without a word. Only a while later did she
say, "I've never seen such a thing."

"You haven't, eh?" I said. I smiled and bucked up, making
as if I'd played my prank for some particular reason, as if there
was something behind it. But what could there be behind it?
For the first time the Doctor looked at me with contempt.

Some time went by; the boats glided homeward, the bad
feeling among the company disappeared, and we sang as we
approached the pier. Edvarda said, "Listen, we haven't finished
the wine, there's quite a lot left. Let's throw another party, a
new party later on; we'll dance, we'll have a ball in our parlor."

When we stepped ashore I apologized to Edvarda.

"How I long to be back in my hut," I said. "This has been
a painful day."

"Has it been a painful day for you, Lieutenant?"

"I mean," I said, dodging the question, "I mean I was a
nuisance both to myself and others. I threw your shoe into the
water."

"Yes, that was an odd thing to do."

"Forgive me!" I said.

XVI

How much worse could things be? I decided to keep my composure whatever happened, as God is my witness. Had I perhaps forced myself upon her from the very first? No, no, never;
our paths just happened to cross one day as she passed by. What

a summer they had here up north! Already the cockchafers had ceased flying, and people were becoming more and more obscure to me, although the sun shed light on them night and day. What were their blue eyes looking for, and what were they thinking behind their strange brows? No matter, they were all of no interest to me anyway. I took my lines and went fishing for two days, four days; but at night I lay with open eyes in my hut. . . .

"Edvarda, I haven't seen you for four days."

"Four days, that's right. You see, I've been busy. Come and look."

She led me into the parlor. The tables had been taken out, the chairs placed along the walls, every article moved; the chandelier, the stove and the walls had been fancifully decorated with heather and black cloths from the store. The piano stood in the corner.

These were her preparations for the "ball."

"What do you think of it?" she asked.

"Wonderful," I said.

We left the room.

"But listen, Edvarda," I said, "have you quite forgotten me?"

"I don't understand you," she answered, surprised. "Didn't you see all I had done? So how could I've come to you?"

"No," I echoed her, "maybe you couldn't come to me." I was heavy-eyed and exhausted, my speech became inane and unguarded, I had been miserable all day. "No, then you couldn't come to me, of course. But what I wanted to say: in a word, there has been a change, something has gotten in the way. Oh yes. But I cannot tell from your face what it is. What a strange forehead you have, Edvarda. I can see that now."

"But I haven't forgotten you!" she cried, blushing, and suddenly slipped her arm through mine.

"All right, maybe you haven't forgotten me. But then I don't know what I'm saying. One or the other."

"You'll get an invitation tomorrow. You must dance with me. Oh, how we shall dance!"

"Will you walk me a little way?" I asked.

"Now? No, I can't," she replied. "The Doctor will be here shortly, he's going to help me with something, there's still some work to do. So, you think the room will be all right like this? But don't you think . . ."

A carriage comes to a halt outside.

"The Doctor is driving today, is he?" I said.

"Yes, I sent a man with a horse to fetch him, I wanted—"

"To spare his sick leg, sure. No, let me be off. . . . How do you do, Doctor. Pleased to see you again. Hale and hearty as ever? I hope you'll excuse my buzzing off."

At the foot of the steps I turned around—Edvarda was standing at the window watching me; she was holding back the curtains with both hands to see, her expression was thoughtful. An absurd joy flashes through me, and I quickly put the house behind me, with light feet and dimmed eyes, the gun light as a walking stick in my hand. If I should win her I would become a good person, I thought. Reaching the forest, I thought again, If I should win her I would serve her more tirelessly than anyone else, and even if she proved unworthy, if she took it into her head to demand the impossible of me, I would still do all I could[20] and rejoice that she was mine. . . . I stopped and fell on my knees, and in humility and hope I brushed my tongue against the blades of grass by the roadside, whereupon I got up again.

At last I felt almost certain. Her changed behavior lately was just her way; she had stood watching me as I left, had stood at the window following me with her eyes till I disappeared. What more could she do? My delight completely befuddled me, I was hungry but could no longer feel it.

Aesop ran on ahead of me, a moment later he began to bark. I looked up, a woman with a white kerchief on her head was standing at the corner of the hut. It was Eva, the blacksmith's daughter.

"Hi, Eva!" I called.

She was standing by the tall gray rock, her face all red, sucking her finger.

"So it's you, Eva? What's up?" I asked.

"Aesop has bitten me," she replied, shyly lowering her eyes.

I looked at her finger. She had bitten it herself. A suspicion flashes through my head, and I ask, "Have you been waiting here long?"

"No, not very long," she replied.

And without either of us saying another word, I took her by the hand and led her into the hut.

XVII

I was returning from my fishing trip as usual and showed up at the "ball" with my gun and bag, only I had put on my best leather clothes. It was late when I got to Sirilund, I could hear dancing inside. Shortly there were calls of "Here's the hunter, the Lieutenant!" I was surrounded by some young people who wanted to see my catch, I had shot a brace of sea birds and caught a few haddocks. Edvarda welcomed me with a smile, she had been dancing and was flushed.

"The first dance with me!" she said.

And we danced. No misadventure occurred—I became dizzy but didn't fall. My big boots made a bit of noise, I could hear the noise myself and decided not to dance anymore; I had also made scratches in the floor paint. But how glad I was that I had done nothing worse!

Mr. Mack's two store clerks were there, dancing painstakingly and earnestly, the Doctor joined eagerly in the country-

dances. Besides these gentlemen, there were four youngish
men, sons of the home parish gentry, the Dean and the district
doctor. A stranger, a commercial traveler, had also joined the
party; he distinguished himself by his fine voice and hummed
in time to the music. Once in a while he would spell the ladies
at the piano.

I can no longer recall how the first few hours went by, but
I remember everything from the latter part of the night. The
sun shone red in through the windows the whole time, and
the sea birds were asleep. We had wine and cakes, talked loudly
and sang, and Edvarda's laughter rang fresh and carefree
through the room. But why didn't she have a word for me
anymore? I went over to where she was sitting, wanting to pay
her a compliment as best I could. She was wearing a black
dress, her confirmation dress perhaps, and it was now much
too short for her; but it suited her when she danced and I
wanted to tell her that.

"That black dress—" I began.

But she got up, put her arm around one of her friends and
walked off with her. This happened two or three times. Well,
I thought, what can be done about that? But then why does
she stand by the window following me with a sad look in her
eyes when I leave her? That's her own affair.

A lady asked me to dance. Edvarda was sitting nearby and I
answered in a loud voice, "No, I'm leaving in a moment."

Edvarda gave me a quizzical glance and said, "Leaving? Alas,
no, you're not leaving."

I was taken aback and felt my teeth digging into my lips. I
got up.

"What you said just now seems quite significant to me, Miss
Edvarda," I said darkly, taking a few steps toward the door.

The Doctor blocked my way, and Edvarda herself came
rushing up.

"Don't misunderstand me," she said warmly. "I meant to
say that hopefully you would be the last to leave, the very last.

And besides, it's only one o'clock. . . . Listen," she added, her
eyes sparkling, "you gave our oarsman five dollars for saving
my shoe from drowning. That was much too high a price."
And she laughed heartily and turned around to the company.

I stood there all agape, disarmed and confused.

"You're pleased to joke," I said. "I certainly didn't give your
oarsman five dollars."

"Oh, you didn't?" She opened the door to the kitchen and
called the oarsman in. "You remember our outing to Korholmerne, don't you, Jakob? You saved my shoe when it fell into
the water."

"Sure," Jakob replied.

"And you received five dollars for saving the shoe, didn't
you?"

"Yes, you gave me—"

"Good. You may go."

What does she mean by this trick? I thought. Is she trying
to put me to shame? She won't succeed, I'm not going to blush
for something like that. I said loud and clear, "I must point out
to all of you here that this is either a mistake or a lie. It never
even occurred to me to give the oarsman a five-dollar reward
for your shoe. I ought perhaps to have done it, but so far I
have not."

"Whereupon the dancing continues," she said, wrinkling
her brows. "Why aren't we dancing?"

She owes me an explanation for this, I said to myself, and I
watched out for a chance to speak with her. She went into the
next room and I followed her.

"Skoal!" I said, wanting to drink a glass with her.

"I have nothing in my glass," she answered shortly.

And yet her glass was full and standing in front of her.

"I thought that was your glass?"

"No, it's not mine," she said and, acting engaged, turned to
the person next to her.

"Pardon me, then!" I said.

Several of the guests noticed this little scene.

My heart hissing inside me, I said, offended, "However, you do owe me an explanation—"

She got up, took hold of both my hands and said in an urgent tone of voice, "But not today, not now. I'm so miserable. God, the way you look at me! We were friends once, after all. . . ."

Overwhelmed, I faced about and rejoined the dancers.

Shortly afterward Edvarda also came in; she placed herself by the piano, where the commercial traveler was playing a dance. Her face at that moment was full of a secret sorrow.

"I've never learned how to play," she says, giving me a veiled look. "If I knew that, at least."

I had no reply to that. But my heart flew out to her once more and I asked, "Why have you suddenly become so sad, Edvarda? If you just knew how much pain it gives me."

"I don't know why," she replied. "Because of everything, perhaps. If only these people would leave at once, one and all. No, not you; remember, you must be the last to leave."

And again her words revived me, and my eyes saw the light in the sun-filled room. The Dean's daughter came over and began talking to me, I wished her ever so far away and gave her short answers. I purposely didn't look at her, since she had spoken about my animal eyes. Turning to Edvarda, she told her how, once abroad—in Riga, I think it was—she had been pursued by a man in the street.

"He kept following me down one street after another and smiling at me," she said.

"Was he blind, then?" I exclaimed, to please Edvarda. I gave a shrug as well.

The young lady caught the drift of my rude words at once and replied, "He certainly must've been, to chase an ugly old woman like me."

But I obtained no gratitude from Edvarda, she pulled her

friend away; they whispered together and shook their heads. From now on I was left entirely to myself.

Another hour goes by, the seabirds begin to wake out by the skerries, their cries reach us through the open windows. A stab of joy went through me at hearing those first bird cries, and I longed to be out there by the skerries. . . .

The Doctor was again in a good humor and drew everybody's attention to himself, the ladies never tired of his company. Can that be my rival? I thought to myself, and I also thought of his lame leg and sorry figure. He had acquired a new and witty oath, he said 'By Jack and Jove,' and each time he used this curious oath I laughed aloud. In my anguish it occurred to me to give this man every advantage I could, since he was my rival. I let it be the Doctor here and the Doctor there, crying, "Listen to what the Doctor is saying!" and I forced myself to laugh aloud at his commonplaces.

"I love this world," the Doctor said, "I cling to life tooth and nail. And when the time comes to die, I hope I'll have a place in eternity somewhere directly above London or Paris, so that I can hear the pandemonium of the human cancan all the time, all the time."

"Splendid!" I cried, coughing from laughter, though I wasn't the least bit intoxicated.

Edvarda, too, seemed to be carried away.

When the guests were leaving I slipped into the small side room and sat down to wait. I could hear one goodbye after another out on the front steps. The Doctor also took his leave and went off. Soon all the voices died away. My heart beat violently as I waited.

Edvarda came back in. When she saw me she stopped a moment in surprise, before she said, smiling, "Oh, there you are! It was kind of you to wait till the last. Now I'm dead tired."

She remained standing.

Getting up, I said, "Yes, you can use some rest now. I hope your despondency has passed, Edvarda. You were so sad a little while back, and it gave me pain."

"It will pass when I get some sleep."

I had no more to add and walked to the door.

"Well, thanks for a pleasant evening," she said, giving me her hand. When she wanted to walk me out, I tried to avert it.

"No need," I said, "don't bother, I can very well find my—"

But she walked me out anyway. She stood there in the hall-way, waiting patiently while I found my cap, my gun and my bag. There was a walking stick in the corner, I saw the stick quite clearly; I stared at it and recognized it—it was the Doctor's. When she notices the direction of my glance she turns red with embarrassment; it was plain to see from her face that she was innocent and knew nothing about the stick. A whole minute goes by. At last a furious impatience flares up in her and she says quiveringly, "Your stick. Do not forget your stick."

And before my very eyes she hands me the Doctor's stick.

I looked at her—she was still holding the stick out, her hand trembling. To make an end of it, I took the stick and put it back in the corner. I said, "It's the Doctor's stick. I can't understand how that lame man could forget his stick."

"You and your lame man!" she cried bitterly, taking another step toward me. "You're not lame, no, but even if you were lame, on top of everything, you couldn't hold your own against him; no, you couldn't, you couldn't hold your own against him. There!"

I searched for some answer but drew a blank, I was silent. With a deep bow, I walked backward out through the door and onto the steps. Here I stood for a moment staring straight in front of me before I wandered off.

So, he has forgotten his stick, I thought, and he'll come back this way to pick it up. He won't let *me* be the last to leave the house. . . . I strolled quite slowly up the road, keeping a lookout, and stopped at the edge of the forest. Finally, after half an hour's wait, the Doctor came walking toward me; he had seen me and walked rapidly. Even before he had time to speak, I raised my cap to test him. He raised his hat as well. I went straight up to him and said, "I didn't greet you."

He backed off a step and stared at me.

"You didn't greet me?"

"No," I said.

Pause.

"Well, it's all the same to me what you did," he replied, blanching. "I was going to pick up my stick, which I left behind."

I had nothing to say to that, but I revenged myself in a different way. I held out my gun to him, as if he were a dog, and said, "Jump over!"

And I whistled and wheedled to make him jump over.

He wrestled with himself for a moment, his face assuming the strangest expressions while he pressed his lips together and kept his eyes fixed on the ground. Suddenly he looked intently at me, a half-smile lighting up his features, and said, "Why are you really doing all this?"

I didn't answer, but his words affected me.

All of a sudden he held out his hand to me and said in a low voice, "There's something wrong with you. If you'll tell me what it is, perhaps . . ."

At this I was overwhelmed by shame and despair, thrown off balance by his calm words. Wanting to make it up to him, I put my arm around him and exclaimed, "Listen, you must forgive me! No, what should be wrong with me? There's nothing wrong, I don't need your help. Maybe you're looking for Edvarda? You'll find her at home. But hurry up, or she'll go to bed before you get there; she was very tired, I saw it myself. This is the best I can tell you, it's true. You'll find her at home, just go!"

And I turned and hurried away from him, rushing with long strides up through the forest and back to my hut.

For a while I sat on my bed in exactly the same state I had come in, my bag over my shoulder and the gun in my hand. Strange thoughts stirred in my head. Why had I given myself away to the Doctor, anyway? I felt mortified at having put my arm around him and looked at him with tears in my eyes; he would gloat over it, I thought, perhaps he's snickering over it with Edvarda at this very moment. He had left his stick in the hallway. No, even if I were lame on top of everything, I couldn't hold my own against the Doctor, could I? I definitely wouldn't be able to hold my own against him, those were her own words. . . .

Standing in the middle of the floor, I cock my gun, place the muzzle against my left instep and pull the trigger. The shot pierces the middle of my foot and goes through the floor. Aesop gives a short, frightened yelp.

Shortly afterward there's a knock on the door.

It was the Doctor who came.

"Pardon me if I disturb you," he began. "You went off so quickly, I thought it wouldn't hurt if we talked a bit. A smell of powder, isn't there?"

He was perfectly sober.

"Did you see Edvarda? Did you get your stick?" I asked.

"I got my stick. No, Edvarda had gone to bed. . . . What's that? But for heaven's sake, you're bleeding!"

"No, next to nothing. I was going to put away my gun and it went off; it's no big deal. Damn you, why should I have to sit here and give you information about this? . . . So, you got your stick?"

He was staring fixedly at my shattered boot and the flow of

blood. With a quick movement he put down his stick and rid himself of his gloves.

"Sit still, your boot has to come off," he said. "It was a shot I heard all right, just as I thought."

XVIII

How I later came to regret that insane shot! The whole affair didn't amount to very much, nor was it good for anything, it just tied me down to the hut for several weeks. All the vexations and inconveniences are still vividly present to my mind; my washerwoman had to come to my hut every day and stay around almost permanently, shop for food and take care of the housekeeping. Several weeks went by. Oh, well!

One day the Doctor began talking about Edvarda. I heard her name, heard what she had said and done, and it was no longer of any great importance to me; it was as though he were talking about something remote that didn't concern me. How quickly one can forget! I thought, astonished at myself.

"Well, what's your own opinion of Edvarda, since you ask? To tell the truth, I haven't thought about her for several weeks. Wait a bit, it seems to me there was something between you two, you were so often together; you were host on an outing to the islands, and she was hostess. Don't deny it, Doctor, there was something, a certain understanding. No, for God's sake, don't answer me, you owe me no explanation, I'm not asking in order to learn anything; let's talk about something else, if you like. When can I walk on my foot again?"

I sat there thinking of what I had said. Why was I afraid, deep down, that the Doctor might express his opinion? What was Edvarda to me? I had forgotten her.

Later the subject of Edvarda came up again, and once more

I interrupted the Doctor. God only knows what it was I dreaded to hear.

"Why are you interrupting me?" he asked. "Can't you stand hearing me utter her name?"

"Tell me," I said, "what's your honest opinion of Miss Edvarda? I would be interested to know."

He gave me a suspicious look. "My honest opinion?"

"Perhaps you have some news to tell me today, you may even have asked for her hand and been accepted. May I congratulate you? No? Well, I'm damned if I believe you, ha-ha-ha!"

"So that's what you were afraid of!"

"Afraid of? My good Doctor!"

Pause.

"No," he said, "I have not asked for her hand and been accepted; perhaps you have. One doesn't ask for Edvarda's hand, she takes whomever she has a fancy for. Do you think she's just a peasant lass? You've been in the company of this person up here, in Nordland, and have seen for yourself. She's a child who hasn't been birched sufficiently, and a woman of many whims. Cold? No fear. Warm? Ice, I tell you. What is she then? A little girl of sixteen or seventeen, right? But just try to influence this little girl and she'll scoff at all your pains. Even her father can't manage her; to all appearance she obeys him, but in reality she's her own mistress. She says that you have animal eyes—"

"You're wrong, it's someone else who says I've got animal eyes."

"Someone else? Who?"

"I don't know. One of her girl friends. No, it's not Edvarda who says that. Just a moment, perhaps it's really Edvarda herself. . . ."

"When you look at her, it has such and such an effect on her, she says. But do you think that brings you a hairsbreadth closer to her? Hardly. Just look at her, don't spare your eyes;

but as soon as she notices she's susceptible to you she'll say to herself, Come, that man who stands over there looking at me thinks he has won the game, doesn't he? And with a single glance, or a cold word, she'll send you a hundred miles away. Do you think I don't know her? How old do you suppose she is?"

"She was born in thirty-eight, wasn't she?"

"A lie. I checked it out, just for the fun of it. She's twenty years old, though she could easily pass for fifteen. She's not a happy soul, there's a lot of fighting going on in that little head of hers. When she's looking out at the mountains or the sea and her mouth takes on a certain expression, an expression of pain, then she's miserable; but she's too proud and too head-strong to cry. She's quite adventurous and has an ardent imag-ination, she's waiting for a prince. What was that story of a certain five-dollar bill you were supposed to have given away?"

"A joke. No, that was nothing—"

"That, too, was something. She did something similar to me once. It's a year ago now. We were aboard the packet boat while it lay in port. It was cold and raining. A woman with a small child sits freezing on deck. Edvarda asks her, 'Aren't you cold?' Oh yes, the woman was cold. 'Isn't the little one cold too?' Oh yes, the little one was cold too. 'Why don't you go into the cabin?' Edvarda asks. 'I travel steerage,' the woman replied. Edvarda looks at me. 'The woman has only a steerage ticket,' she says. What can we do about it? I reply inwardly. But I understand Edvarda's look. I was not born wealthy, I've worked my way up from nothing, and I count the money I give out. And so I move away from the woman, thinking, If anyone is to pay for her, then let Edvarda herself pay, she and her father can better afford it than I. And, sure enough, Edvarda pays. In that respect she's wonderful, she doesn't lack a heart. But as sure as I'm sitting here, she had expected me to pay for a cabin for the woman and her little one, I could tell by the look in her eyes. What happened then? The woman got up and thanked her for her great help. 'Don't thank me, but thank that gentleman over there,' Edvarda answered, pointing at me without batting an eye. What do you think of that? I hear the woman thanking me too, but can think of nothing to say in reply, I must let things take their course. Well, that's just one episode, but I could relate several. And as for those five dollars to the oarsman, she gave him the money herself. If you had done it, she would have thrown her arms around your neck: you should have been the gallant who committed that extravagant absurdity for the sake of a worn-out shoe, it would've suited her ideas, she had decided on it. When you didn't do it, she did it herself, in your name. That's the way she is, at once unreasonable and calculating."

"So, can't anybody win her then?" I asked.

"She should be taken in hand," the Doctor replied, evasively. "There's something wrong here, she has a too free rein; she can do anything she wants and carry the day whenever she likes. People make much of her, she's never given the cold shoulder; there's always someone at hand whom she can impress. Have you noticed how I treat her? Like a schoolgirl, a little wench; I hector her, find fault with her speech, pay attention and put her on the spot. Do you think she doesn't understand? Ah, she's proud and stubborn, it hurts her every time; but then again she's too proud to show that it hurts her. Anyway, that's how she should be handled. When you came I'd already been taking her in hand for a year and it was beginning to work; she would cry with pain and vexation, but she had become a more reasonable person. Then you came along and ruined it all. That's the way it is—one lets her go and another picks her up again. After you, I daresay there will be a third, who knows."

Oho, I thought, the Doctor wants to get back at her for something, and I said, "Now tell me, Doctor, why have you gone to the trouble and inconvenience of telling me all this? Am I supposed to help you take Edvarda in hand?"

"By the way, she's as hot as a volcano," he continued, without heeding my question. "You asked if anybody could ever win her. Oh sure, why not? She's waiting for her prince, he hasn't come yet, she makes one mistake after another; she also thought that you were the prince, especially since you had animal eyes, ha-ha. Look, Lieutenant, you ought to have brought your uniform, at least. It would have been of some importance now. Why shouldn't somebody be able to win her? I've seen her wringing her hands for someone who might come and take her, carry her off, rule over her body and soul. Yes. But he must come from the outside, pop up some day as a rather special being. I have a hunch that Mr. Mack is away on an expedition, I dare say there's something behind that trip of his. Mr. Mack went on a trip once before too, and when he returned there was a gentleman with him."

"There was a gentleman with him?"

"Alas, he was no good," the Doctor said, with a pained laugh. "He was a man about my own age, he limped too, just like me. He was not the prince."

"And where did he go?" I asked, looking intently at the Doctor.

"Where he went? From here? I don't know," he answered, confused. "Well, we have dwelt on this much too long. You can begin to walk on your foot in a week or so. See you later."

XIX

I hear a woman's voice outside my hut. The blood rushes to my head, it's Edvarda's voice.

"Glahn! Glahn is sick, I hear?"

And my washerwoman answers outside the door, "He's almost well again now."

That "Glahn, Glahn!" pierced me to the quick; she uttered my name twice, it touched me, her voice was clear and tremulous.

She opened the door without knocking, stepped hurriedly in and looked at me. Suddenly it seemed like in the old days again, she was wearing her dyed jacket and had tied her pinafore rather low to have a long waist. I saw it all at once, and the look in her eyes, her brown face with the eyebrows high up on her forehead, the strangely tender expression of her hands—everything hit me so forcefully, it made me confused. Her I have kissed! I thought. I got up and just stood there.

"You're getting up, you can stand!" she said. "But sit down, your foot is bad, you shot yourself. Good God, how did it happen? I just found out about it. I kept thinking the whole time, What has become of Glahn? He never comes anymore. I didn't know anything. You had shot yourself, several weeks ago now, I hear, and I knew nothing about it. How do you feel now? You've become terribly pale, I barely recognize you. And your foot? Will you be lame? The Doctor says you won't be lame. Oh, how dearly I love you, that you won't be lame, I thank God for it. I hope you'll forgive me for coming here just like this, I ran more than I walked. . . ."

She bent over toward me, she was so close to me, I felt her breath on my face and reached out my hands for her. Then she moved further away. Her eyes were still moist.

"It happened like this," I stammered. "I wanted to put the gun away in the corner but was holding it incorrectly, like this, the wrong end up; then suddenly I heard a shot. It was an accident."

"An accident," she said thoughtfully and nodded. "Let me see, it's your left foot; but why just the left? Well, it happened by chance—"

"Yes, by chance," I cut in. "How can I know why it turned out to be just the left foot? You can see for yourself—I was holding the gun like this, so it couldn't very well be the right foot. Well, it wasn't very much fun."

She looked thoughtfully at me.

"Anyway, you're recovering very nicely," she said, looking about her in the hut. "Why didn't you send the woman over to us for food? What have you been living on?"

We talked for another few minutes. I said to her, "When you came your face was warm and your eyes shone, you gave me your hand. Now your eyes are indifferent again. Am I wrong?"

Pause.

"One cannot always be the same."

"Tell me just this once," I said: "What have I said or done this time, for example, to displease you? It might give me something to go by in the future."

She looked out of the window, toward the far horizon; she stood and looked pensively in front of her, answering me who sat behind her, "Nothing, Glahn. One cannot help having one's own thoughts sometimes, you know. Are you dissatisfied now? Remember, some give little and it's a lot for them, others give all and it costs them no great effort. Who, then, has given the most? You've become melancholy during your illness. How did we get to talk about this anyway?" And suddenly she looks at me, her face suffused with joy, and says, "Get well soon, will you. Till we meet again."

With that she gave me her hand.

Then I took it into my head not to accept her hand. I stood up, put my hands behind my back and made a deep bow; by this I meant to thank her for her kind visit.

"Sorry I can't walk you any further," I said.

When she had gone, I set about thinking it all over once more. I wrote a letter asking for my uniform to be sent me.

XX

The first day in the forest.

I was happy and faint, the animals came up close and looked me over, there were beetles on the leafy trees and blister beetles crawling on the path. Hello there! I thought. The mood of the forest flowed back and forth through my senses, I wept for love of it and was perfectly happy, dissolved in thanksgiving. Sweet forest, my home, may God's peace be with you, it comes straight from my heart. . . . I stop, turn in all directions and, weeping, call birds, trees, rocks, grass, and ants by name, I look about me and name them one after the other. I look up toward the mountains and think, Yes, I'm coming! as if answering a call. There, high up, the merlin nested, I knew of its nests. But the thought of the nesting merlins up in the mountains took my fantasy far away.

Around noon I rowed out and landed on a small island, a rock out beyond the harbor. There were lilac-colored flowers on long stems that reached to my knees, I waded through strange vegetation, raspberry bushes, coarse goose grass. There were no animals there, nor may there ever have been any people. The sea foamed gently against the islet, enfolding me in a veil of murmurings; way up by the nesting rocks the shore birds were all flying about screaming. But the sea enclosed me on every side, like an embrace. Blessed be life and earth and sky, blessed be my enemies—in this hour I would show mercy to my worst enemy and tie his shoelaces. . . .

A loud hoisting shanty reaches me from one of Mr. Mack's fishing smacks, and my heart is filled with sunshine at the familiar sound. I row back to the pier, pass the fishermen's shacks and go home. The day is over, I have my meal, sharing my food with Aesop, and set out for the woods once more. A soft wind wafts against my face without a sound. May you be blessed, I say to the winds, because they blow upon my face, may you be blessed; the blood in my veins bows down to you in thanksgiving! Aesop puts his paw on my knee.

Weariness overcomes me and I fall asleep.

Ding-dong! Bells ringing? Some miles out to sea stands a mountain. I say two prayers, one for my dog and one for myself, and we enter the mountain. The gate slams behind us, I give a start and wake up.

A flaming red sky, the sun throbs before my eyes, the night, the horizon, resonates with light. Aesop and I go into the shade. It's quiet all around. "No, we won't sleep anymore," I say to Aesop, "we're going hunting tomorrow, that red sun is shining on us, we didn't enter the mountain. . . ." And quaint moods quicken in me, and the blood rushes to my head. Excited but still weak, I feel someone kissing me, and the kiss lingers on my lips. I look about me, there's no one to be seen. Iselin! I say. There's a rustle in the grass, it could be leaves falling to the ground, it could also be footsteps. A shudder sweeps through the forest—that could be Iselin's breath, I think. In these woods Iselin has wandered, here she has answered the prayers of hunters, in their yellow boots and green cloaks. She lived on her estate a few miles from here; four generations ago, she sat by her window and heard the hunting-horn echo from the forests round about. There were reindeer and wolves and bears, and the hunters were many; and they all saw her grow up, and each and every one waited for her. One had seen her eyes, another had heard her voice; but once a sleepless young man got up at night and bored a hole to Iselin's chamber, and he saw her white velvet body. In her twelfth year Dundas came. He was a Scotsman trading in fish, owner of many ships. He had a son. When Iselin was sixteen, she saw young Dundas for the first time. He was her first love. . . .

And such quaint moods flow through me, and my head grows heavy as I sit there; I close my eyes and again feel Iselin's kiss. Iselin, are you there, you life's darling? I say, and do you let Diderik stand behind a tree? . . . But my head feels heavier and heavier, and I'm carried away on the waves of sleep.[21]

Ding-dong! A voice speaks, it is as if the Pleiades were singing in my blood, it's Iselin's voice.

Sleep, sleep! I'll tell you about my love while you sleep, and I'll tell you about my first night. I remember how I forgot to lock my door; I was sixteen, it was spring with warm winds; Dundas came. It was as if an eagle came swooping down. I met him one morning before the hunt, he was twenty-five and just back from distant travels; he walked by my side in the garden, and when he brushed me with his arm I began loving him. Two fever-red spots broke out on his forehead, and I could have kissed those two spots.

In the evening after the hunt I went to look for him in the garden, and I was afraid lest I should find him. I spoke his name softly to myself, and I was afraid[22] lest he should hear me. Then he steps out from the bushes and whispers, Tonight at one o'clock! Whereupon he disappears.

Tonight at one, I say to myself, what did he mean by that? I don't understand. He probably meant that he was going away again tonight at one, but what is it to me if he goes away?

And that was how I forgot to lock my door. . . .

At one o'clock he comes in.

Wasn't my door locked? I ask.

I'll lock it, he says.

And he locks the door and shuts us in.

I was anxious about the noise of his heavy boots. Don't wake up my maid! I said. I was also anxious about the creaking chair, and I said, No, no, don't sit on that chair, it creaks!

May I sit with you on the sofa, then? he asked.

Yes, I said.

But that I said only because the chair creaked.

We sat on the sofa. I moved away, he moved up. I lowered my eyes.

You're cold, he said, taking my hand. Shortly after he said, How cold you are! and put his arm around me.

I grew warm in his arm. We sit like this awhile. A cock crows.

Did you hear? he said, a cock crowed, it'll soon be morning.

And he touched me and I was lost.

As long as you're quite sure that the cock crowed, I stammered.

Again I saw those two fever-red spots on his forehead, and I tried to get up. Then he held me back, I kissed the two lovable spots and closed my eyes for him. . . .

Then the day came, already it was morning. I awoke and didn't recognize the walls of my chamber, I got up and didn't recognize my own little shoes; something rippled through me. What can it be that ripples through me? I thought, laughing. And what hour did the clock strike just now? I knew nothing, I remembered only I had forgotten to lock my door.

My maid comes.

Your flowers haven't been watered, she says.

I had forgotten my flowers.

You have rumpled your dress, she goes on.

Where can I have rumpled my dress? I wonder, with a laugh in my heart; but I guess I must have done it last night.

A carriage drives up to the garden gate.

And your cat hasn't been fed, says my maid.

But I forget my flowers, my dress and my cat and ask, Is that Dundas stopping outside? Ask him to come to me at once, I'm expecting him, there was something . . . something . . . And I think to myself, Will he lock the door again when he comes?

He knocks. I open to him and lock the door myself, to do him a small favor.

Iselin! he exclaims and kisses my lips for a full minute.

I didn't send for you, I whisper.

You didn't? he asks.

Again I'm quite lost and I answer, Yes, I did send for you, I longed so unspeakably for you again. Stay here awhile.

And I held my hands before my eyes for love. He didn't let me go, I swooned and hid myself on his breast.

I think I hear something crowing again, he said, listening.

But when I heard what he said, I cut him off as quickly as I could and replied, Why, how can you think something is crowing again! There wasn't any crowing.

He kissed my bosom.

It was only the crowing of a hen, I said at the last moment.

Wait a little, I'll lock the door, he said, about to rise.

I held him back and whispered, It's locked. . . .

Then it was evening again and Dundas was gone. A golden ripple went through me. I stood before the mirror and two enamored eyes looked out at me; something stirred within me at my glance, and I felt one ripple after another around my heart. Good God, I had never looked at myself with those eyes before, and I gave my own lips an amorous kiss in the mirror. . . .

And now I have told you about my first night and about the morning and evening thereafter. Some other time I'll tell you about Svend Herlufsen. I loved him too, he lived six miles from here, on the island you can see out there, and on calm summer nights I used to row out to him, because I loved him. I'll also tell you about Stamer. He was a pastor, and I loved him. I love all. . . .

Through my slumber I hear a cock crowing down at Sirilund.

Did you hear, Iselin, a cock crowed for us too! I cry joyfully, stretching out my arms. I wake up. Aesop is already on his legs. Gone! I say in burning sorrow and look about me. There's no one here, no one! Hot and excited, I walk homeward. It's morning, and the cock continues to crow down at Sirilund.

By the hut stands a woman, it's Eva. She has a rope in her hand and is going to fetch firewood. The young girl has an aura of life's first morning, her breast rises and falls, the sun scatters gold on her.

"Don't imagine . . . ," she stammers.

"What mustn't I imagine, Eva?"

"I didn't come this way to meet you, I was just passing by. . . ."

And her face darkens with a blush.

XXI

My foot continued to give me trouble and pain, it often itched at night and kept me awake; sudden twinges would shoot through it, and when the weather changed it was full of rheumatism. It lasted for many days. But I wouldn't have a limp.

The days went by.

Mr. Mack had returned, as I would learn to my cost in no time. He took my boat away, putting me in an awkward situation; it wasn't yet open season and there was nothing I could shoot. But why did he deprive me of the boat like that? Two of Mr. Mack's dock workers had rowed a stranger out to sea in the morning.

I met the Doctor.

"They've taken my boat away," I said.

"A visitor has arrived," he said. "They have to row him out to sea every day and bring him back again in the evening. He's investigating the seabed."

The visitor was a Finlander, Mr. Mack had met him by chance on the ship; he came from Spitsbergen with some collections of shells and small marine animals. They called him

Baron. He had been given a large salon as well as another room in Mr. Mack's house. He attracted much attention.

Being in want of meat, I thought I could ask Edvarda for a bit of food for the evening. I stroll down to Sirilund. I notice right away that Edvarda is wearing a new dress, she seems to have grown, her dress is very long.

"Pardon me for not getting up," she said briefly, giving me her hand.

"Yes, I'm afraid my daughter is indisposed," Mr. Mack said. "It's a cold, she has been careless. . . . I suppose you've come to find out about your boat? I'll have to lend you another one, a four-oar; it's not new, but as long as you keep bailing . . . You see, we have a scientist in the house, and you'll understand that a man like that . . . He has no time to spare, he works all day and comes home in the evening. Don't go now before he comes and you can meet him, it will interest you to make his acquaintance. Here's his card, with a coronet: Baron. A charming man. I met him quite by chance."

Aha, I thought, you won't be invited for supper. Well, thank goodness, I came here just to test the waters, I can go home again, there's still some fish left in the hut. I'll get up a meal somehow. That's that.

The Baron came. A small man of around forty, with a long, narrow face, prominent cheekbones and a sparse black beard. He had piercing gimlet eyes, but he used strong glasses. He had the same five-pointed coronet on his studs as on his card. He was slightly stooped and his thin hands were blue-veined; but his nails looked as if made of yellow metal.

"Pleased to meet you, Lieutenant. Have you been here long?"

"A few months."

A pleasant man. Mr. Mack urged him to tell us about his shells and his marine animals, and this he did willingly; he explained to us the kind of clay there was around Korholmerne and went into the salon and fetched a sample of seaweed from the White Sea. He was constantly raising his right forefinger to move his thick gold-rimmed glasses up and down his nose. Mr. Mack was greatly interested. An hour went by.

The Baron spoke about my accident, my unfortunate shot. Was I well again now? Really? Pleased to hear it.

Who has told him about my accident? I thought. I asked, "From whom did you hear about my accident, Baron?"

"From—well, who was it now? Miss Mack, I believe. Isn't that so, Miss Mack?"

Edvarda turned flaming red.

I had come there so poor, weighed down for several days by a dark despair, but at the stranger's last words an instant joy fluttered through me. I didn't look at Edvarda, but I thought, Thanks for speaking of me anyway, for framing my name with your lips, though it is for ever unimportant to you. Good night.

I took my leave. Edvarda remained seated as before, excusing herself for the sake of politeness by saying she was indisposed. She gave me her hand with indifference.

And Mr. Mack was chatting eagerly with the Baron. He was talking about his grandfather, Consul Mack: "I don't know whether I've already told you, Baron, that this clip was pinned to my grandfather's breast by King Carl Johan's own hands."

I came onto the front steps, nobody had seen me out. When I glanced in through the windows of the parlor in passing, there stood Edvarda, tall, erect, parting the curtains with both hands and looking out. I neglected bowing to her—I forgot everything, caught by a torrent of confusion that carried me swiftly away.

Halt, stop a moment! I said to myself when I had reached the forest. By God in heaven, this must end! Suddenly I was hot with anger and groaned. Alas, there was no honor in my breast anymore; I had enjoyed Edvarda's favor for a week at most, it was now long past, but I had failed to act accordingly. From now on my heart would cry at her, Dust, air, dirt on my way, by God in heaven. . . .

I reached the hut, took out my fish and had a meal.

Here you are, burning your life out on account of a wretched little schoolgirl, and your nights are full of empty dreams. And a sultry wind clings to your head, a stinking year-old wind. While the sky trembles with the most wonderful blue and the mountains are calling. Come Aesop, hey!

XXII

A week went by. I hired the blacksmith's boat and went fishing for my dinner. Edvarda and the visiting Baron were always together in the evening when he returned from the sea, I saw them once at the mill. One evening they both came walking past my hut, I drew back from the window and gently closed my door, just in case. It didn't affect me at all to see them together; I just shrugged my shoulder. Another evening[23] I came across them on the road and we bowed to one another; I let the Baron greet me first, and then just touched my cap with a couple of fingers, to be discourteous.[24] I walked slowly past, looking indifferently at them as I did so.

Another day went by.

Oh, all those long days that had now gone by! I was prey to a mood of dejection, my heart given to an aimless brooding; even the friendly gray rock by my hut seemed to sit there with an expression of pain and despair when I walked by. Rain was brewing, the heat was positively gasping before me wherever I turned, my left foot was rheumatic, and I had seen one of Mr. Mack's horses shake himself in his harness in the morning. All these things had a meaning to me as weather signs.[25] I'd better stock up on food while the weather holds, I thought.

I tied up Aesop, took my fishing gear and my gun and went down to the pier. I felt unusually heavy at heart.

"When does the packet boat get here?" I asked a fisherman.

"The packet boat? It'll be here in about three weeks," he replied.

"I'm expecting my uniform," I said.

Then I met one of Mr. Mack's store clerks. I took his hand and said, "Tell me, for Jesus' sake, don't you ever play whist at Sirilund anymore?"

"Oh yes, often," he replied.

Pause.

"I haven't been able to make it lately," I said.

I rowed out to my fishing grounds. The weather had become oppressive and the mosquitoes gathered in swarms, I had to smoke all the time to protect myself. The haddock were biting; I fished with double hooks and made a good catch. On the way back I shot a brace of razorbills.

When I got to the pier the blacksmith was there. He was working. Struck by a thought, I ask him, "Coming up my way?"

"No," he says, "Mr. Mack has given me a job to do that'll keep me busy till midnight."

I nodded, thinking to myself that this was good.

I took my catch and made off, going around by the blacksmith's house. Eva was home alone.

"I've been longing for you with all my heart," I said to her. And I was moved at the sight of her, she could barely look at me for surprise. "I love your youth and your kind eyes," I said. "But today you must punish me for thinking more about someone else than about you. Listen, I've come here just to look at you, it does me good, I love you. Did you hear me calling you last night?"

"No," she replied, dismayed.

"I called Edvarda, Miss Edvarda, but I meant you. I woke up from it. Oh yes, I meant you, I can explain it; I made a slip of the tongue when I said Edvarda. But let's not talk about her anymore. My God, Eva, aren't you my dearest girl, though!

You have such red lips today. You have more beautiful feet than Edvarda, just see for yourself." I lifted up her dress and showed her her own legs.

A joy the like of which I'd never seen in her before flits across her face; she is about to turn away, but hesitates and throws her arm around my neck.

Some time goes by. We talk, sitting all the while on a long bench and talking to each other about many things. I said, "Can you believe it, Miss Edvarda hasn't learned to speak yet, she talks like a child, saying 'more happier,' I've heard it myself. Do you think she has an attractive forehead? I don't. She has a devilish[26] forehead. And she doesn't wash her hands either."

"But we weren't going to talk about her anymore."

"Right. I just forgot."

Some time passes again. I'm thinking of something and fall silent.

"Why are you getting tears in your eyes?" Eva asks.

"Come to think, she does have an attractive forehead," I say, "and her hands are always clean. It was only by chance that they were dirty once. That was all I meant to say." But then I continue angrily and with clenched teeth, "I'm constantly thinking of you, Eva; but it occurs to me that perhaps you haven't heard what I'm going to tell you now. The first time Edvarda saw Aesop she said, 'Aesop? He was a sage, right? He was a Phrygian!' Isn't it just ridiculous? I bet she'd read it in a book the same day."

"Yes," Eva says, "and what then?"

"As far as I recall she also mentioned that Aesop had Xanthus for his teacher. Ha-ha-ha!"

"Really!"

"What the hell is the point of telling the company that Aesop had Xanthus for his teacher, anyway? I'm just asking. Ah, you're not in the right mood today, Eva, or you would laugh yourself sick over it."

"No, I too think it's funny," Eva says, breaking into a

strained, surprised laugh. "But I don't understand it as well as you do."

I hold my peace and ponder, hold my peace and ponder.

"Would you, rather, that we just sit still and don't talk," Eva asks softly. Kindness shone in her eyes, she passed her hand over my hair.

"You good, kind soul!" I exclaim, pressing her ardently to my breast. "I swear I'll die for love of you, I love you more and more, in the end you'll come with me when I leave. Just wait and see. Could you come with me?"

"Yes," she answers.

I can barely hear this yes, but I feel it in her breath, it's written all over her; we hold each other in a wild embrace and she gives herself to me with abandon.

About an hour later I kiss Eva goodbye and leave. At the door I meet Mr. Mack.

Mr. Mack himself.

He gives a start and stares into the room, just stands there on the doorstep staring. "Well, well!" he says, unable to utter another word; he seems knocked into a daze.

"You hadn't expected to find me here?" I say, nodding to him.

Eva doesn't budge.

Mr. Mack collects himself, a remarkable confidence settles on him and he replies, "You're mistaken, you're the very person I'm looking for. I wish to call to your attention that from the first of April to the fifteenth of August it's forbidden to fire a gun within three quarters of a mile of the bird rocks and the down-gathering sites. You shot two birds out at the island today, you were seen by some people."

"I shot two razorbills," I said, stricken. I realized on the spot that the man was within his rights.

"Two razorbills or two eider ducks, it's all the same. You were within a protected area."

"I admit that," I said. "It hasn't occurred to me until now."

"But it ought to have occurred to you."

"I also fired off both barrels at roughly the same place in May. It happened during an outing to the islands. It was done at your own request."

"That's another matter," Mr. Mack said curtly.

"Then you damn well know what you can do!"

"Very well," he replied.

Eva was holding herself in readiness; when I went out she followed me. She had put on a kerchief and walked away from the house, I saw her head for the docks. Mr. Mack went home.

I thought it over. How shrewdly he found a way out! And what gimlet eyes! One shot, two shots, a brace of razorbills, a fine, a payment. And then all, yes all, would be settled with Mr. Mack and his house. Altogether, everything was going very nicely and swiftly. . . .

Already big soft drops of rain began falling. The magpies flew close to the ground, and when I got home and released Aesop, he ate grass. The wind started whistling.

XXIII

Six miles below me I can see the ocean. It's raining and I'm up in the mountains, a cliff is protecting me from the rain. I'm smoking my pipe, smoking one pipe after another, and each time I light up, the tobacco crawls up from the ash like little glowworms. My head swarms with thoughts in the same way. Before me on the ground lies a bundle of dry twigs from a ruined bird's nest. And as that bird's nest, so is also my soul.

I remember every trifle, however small, of this and the following day's happenings. Ho-ho, what a beating I took. . . .

I'm sitting up here in the mountains, amid the roar from the sea and in the air, with the wind and weather seething and wailing horribly in my ears. Far out, fishing smacks and sloops with reefed sails can be seen; there are people on board, bound for somewhere presumably—God knows where all those lives are bound for, I think to myself. The sea rears up in foaming waves and tosses about, tosses about as though peopled by huge, furious creatures flinging their limbs about and roaring at one another. No, it is a festival of ten thousand whistling devils, ducking their heads between their shoulders and circling around, lashing the sea white with their wing tips. Far, far out sits a hidden rock, and from this rock there rises a white merman—he shakes his head at a square-rigged boat that has sprung a leak and is running out to sea before the wind, ho-ho, out to sea, out into the desolate sea. . . .

I am glad to be alone so that no one can see my eyes; I lean trustingly against the rock wall, knowing that no one can watch me from behind. A bird glides over the mountain with a broken cry, while some way off a rock breaks loose and rolls down toward the sea. And I go on quietly sitting there awhile, taking my ease as a warm feeling of contentment thrills through me, because I can sit so secure in my shelter while the rain continues to pour outside. I buttoned up my jacket and thanked God for the warmth of it. Some more time went by. I fell asleep.[27]

It's afternoon, I go home, it's still raining. Then something extraordinary happens to me. Edvarda stands on the path before me. She is drenched, as if she's been out in the rain a long time, but she smiles. What next, I instantly think to myself, seized with indignation! I grip my gun with furious fingers as I walk toward her, although she's smiling.

"Good afternoon!" she calls.

I wait until I've gotten a few steps closer before I say, "I salute you, fair maiden!"

She's taken aback by my facetiousness. Alas, I didn't know what I was saying. She smiles timorously and gazes at me.

"You've been up in the mountains today!" she says. "Then you must be wet. I have a kerchief here, if you'd wrap it around you, I can spare it. . . . No, you refuse to recognize me." And she lowers her eyes and shakes her head because I don't accept the kerchief.[28]

"A kerchief?" I reply, sneering with anger and surprise. "But I have a jacket here, would you like to borrow it? I can spare it, I would've lent it to anyone, so don't worry about taking it. I would gladly have lent it to a fishwife."

I saw she just couldn't wait to hear what I would say, she was listening so eagerly that she grew ugly, letting her mouth gape. There she stands with the kerchief in her hand, a white silk kerchief she has removed from her neck. And I pull off my jacket.

"For God's sake, put it on again!" she cries. "You mustn't do that. Are you that angry with me? Good heavens, put your jacket on again, will you, before you get soaked."

I slipped my jacket on again.

"Where are you going?" I asked listlessly.

"Oh, nowhere. . . . I don't understand how you could pull off your jacket—"

"What have you done with the Baron today?" I went on. "Surely, the Count can't be out at sea in weather like this—"

"Glahn, I just wanted to tell you something—"

I interrupt her, "May I ask you to convey my respects to the Duke?"

We gaze at each other. I'm prepared to meet her with further interruptions if she should open her mouth. Finally a pained expression glides over her face, I look away and say, "Frankly speaking, Miss Edvarda, send that prince about his business. He's not the man for you. I can assure you he's been wondering these last few days whether he should make you his wife or not, and that isn't good enough for you."

"Let's not talk about that, please! Glahn, I've been thinking of you—you could take off your jacket and get soaked for the sake of someone else—I've come to you—"

I shrug my shoulders and go on, "I suggest the Doctor to you instead. What fault can you find with him? A man in his prime, an excellent head. Think about it."

"Listen to me for just a minute—"

"Aesop, my dog, is waiting for me in the hut." I doffed my cap, bowed to her and said again, "I salute you, fair maiden."

With that I started walking away.

She let out a scream. "No, don't tear my heart out of my breast. I've come to you today, I've been on the lookout for you here, and I smiled when you came. Yesterday I went nearly out of my mind because of something I had been thinking of all the time, I was completely at sea and constantly thinking about you. Today as I was sitting in the parlor, someone came in; I didn't look up, but I knew who it was. 'Yesterday I rowed three quarters of a mile,' he said. 'Didn't you get tired?' I asked. 'Alas, yes, very tired, and I got blisters in my hands,' he said, and he fretted over it. I thought, Why, to fret over a thing like that! After a while he said, 'Last night I heard whispering outside my windows, it was your housekeeper and one of your store clerks in intimate conversation.' 'Yes, they're getting married,' I said. 'Yes, but this was at two o'clock in the morning.' 'So what?' I asked, and a moment later I said, 'The night is theirs.' Then he pushed his gold-rimmed glasses further up on his nose and remarked, 'But don't you agree, don't you think it makes a bad impression, in the middle of the night like that?' I still didn't look up, and we sat like that for ten minutes. 'May I bring a shawl to put around your shoulders?' he asked. 'No, thank you,' I replied. 'What if I ventured to take your little hand?' he said. I didn't answer, my thoughts were elsewhere. He placed a small box in my lap, I opened the box and found a brooch in it. There was a coronet on the brooch, and I counted ten precious stones in it. . . . Glahn, I have the brooch right here, would you like to see it? It's trampled to bits, just come here and you'll see it's trampled to bits. . . . 'Well, what am I to do with this brooch?' I asked. 'You shall adorn yourself with it,' he replied. But I handed the brooch back to him and said, 'Let me be, I think more of someone else.' 'Who else?' he asked. 'A hunter,' I said. 'He gave me only two lovely feathers to remember him by, but take your brooch back.' But he refused to take the brooch back. Only then did I look at him, his eyes were piercing. 'I will not take the brooch back, do with it as you wish, step on it,' he said. I stood up, placed the brooch under my heel and stepped on it. That was this morning. . . . I waited for four hours; in the afternoon I went out. He came to meet me on the road. 'Where are you going?' he asked. 'To Glahn,' I replied, 'I'm going to ask him not to forget me. . . .' I've been waiting here since one o'clock, I stood beside a tree and saw you coming, you looked like a god. I loved your figure, your beard and your shoulders, I loved everything about you. . . . Now you're impatient, you want to go—just go, you don't care about me, you aren't even looking at me. . . ."

I had stopped. When she fell silent I began to walk away again. I was worn out with despair and smiled, my heart was hard.

"Come to think," I said and stopped again, "you wanted to tell me something, didn't you?"

This taunt made her tired of me.

"Tell you something? But I have told you something, didn't you hear? No, nothing, I have nothing more to tell you. . . ."

Her voice trembles strangely, but it doesn't touch me.

XXIV

The next morning Edvarda is standing in front of the hut as I step out.

In the course of the night I had thought it all over and made my decision. Why should I let myself be blinded any longer by this capricious person, this fisher wench with her empty head; hadn't her name been stuck in my heart long enough, sucking it dry? Enough of that! Anyway, it occurred to me that I had perhaps got closer to her precisely by acting indifferent and mocking her. Ah, how charmingly I had ridiculed her: after she had made a speech several minutes long I say calmly, Come to think, you wanted to tell me something, didn't you?

She was standing by the rock. Greatly agitated, she was about to run toward me, her arms already outstretched, but she checked herself and just stood there wringing her hands. I touched my cap and bowed to her in silence.

"Today there's only one thing I want of you, Glahn," she said urgently. And I didn't move, just to get to know what she wanted to say. "I hear you've been at the blacksmith's place. In the evening one day. Eva was home alone."

I was taken aback and replied, "From whom have you received that information?"

"I'm not a spy," she cried. "I heard it last night, my father told me. When I came home so soaking wet last night, my father said, 'You insulted the Baron today.' 'No,' I replied. 'Where have you been now?' he then asked. I replied, 'With Glahn.' Then my father told me."

I fight down my despair and say, "Eva has also been here."

"She has been here too? In the hut?"

"Several times. I made her come in. We talked."

"Here too!"

Pause. Stick to your guns! I tell myself, and then I say, "Since you're so kind as to meddle in my affairs, I won't be left behind. Yesterday I proposed the Doctor to you; have you thought it over? The Prince, you see, is just too impossible."

Anger flares up in her eyes.

"He's *not* impossible, I tell you!" she says vehemently. "No, he's far better than you, he can be in a house without smashing cups and glasses, and he leaves my shoes alone. Yes, he knows how to act with people, but you are ridiculous, I'm ashamed of you, you're insufferable, you understand!"

Her words hit home, I bowed my head and replied, "You're right, I don't know very well how to act with people. Show some mercy; you don't understand me, I prefer to stay in the woods, that's my joy. Here in my solitude it does no harm to anyone that I am as I am, but when I get together with others I have to concentrate on being as I ought to. For two years now I've been very little among people—"

"With you one has to be prepared for the worst every moment," she went on. "It gets tiring to look after you in the long run."

How mercilessly she said that! An acute, bitter pang shoots through me, I all but stagger back before her vehemence. But Edvarda hadn't yet done, she added, "Perhaps you can get Eva to look after you. What a pity she's married."

"Eva? Did you say that Eva is married?" I asked.

"Yes, married."

"Who's she married to?"

"You know that, don't you? Eva is married to the blacksmith."

"Isn't she the blacksmith's daughter?"

"No, she's his wife. Do you think I'm lying?"

I had no thoughts on that score, I was simply so astonished. I just stood there thinking, Eva married?

"So you've made a lucky choice, haven't you?" Edvarda says.

Oh, there would never be an end to it all! I started trembling with indignation, and I said, "But do take the Doctor, as I told you. Listen to a friend's advice, that prince of yours is an old fool." And in my exasperation I lied about him, exaggerating his age, saying that he was bald and almost totally blind; I also maintained that the only reason he was wearing that coronet on his studs was to boast of his noble birth. "Incidentally, I haven't taken the trouble to make his acquaintance," I said.

"There's nothing distinctive about him, he lacks the essentials, he's nothing."

"But he *is* something, he *is* something!"[29] she screamed, her voice failing her from anger. "He's much more than you think, you forest tramp! But just you wait! Oh yes, he shall speak to you, I'll ask him to. You don't believe that I love him, but I'll show you that you're mistaken. I'm going to marry him, I'll think about him night and day. Remember what I'm saying: I love him. Just let Eva come—haw-haw, God in heaven, let her just come, I have no words for how little I care. Well, I'd better get away from here. . . ." She started walking down the path from the hut. After a few short, eager steps, she turned around, her face still deathly pale, and groaned, "And don't let me set eyes on you ever again!"

XXV

The leaves were turning yellow, the potato plants had grown tall and were in bloom, the hunting season came round again, I shot ptarmigan, grouse and hare, and one day I shot an eagle. A calm, lofty sky, cool nights, many clear notes and pure[30] sounds in field and forest. The wide world lay in a peaceful repose. . . .

"I have heard nothing more from Mr. Mack about the two razorbills I shot," I said to the Doctor.

"You have Edvarda to thank for that," he said. "I know, I heard her oppose it."

"She will have no thanks from me," I said. . . .

Indian summer, Indian summer. The paths wound like ribbons through the yellowing woods, a new star appeared every day, the moon looked dim as a shadow, a shadow of gold dipped in silver. . . .

"God help you, Eva, you're married, aren't you?"

"Didn't you know?"

"No, I didn't."

She squeezed my hand in silence.

"God help you, child, what shall we do now?"

"Whatever *you* wish. Maybe you won't be leaving yet, I'll be happy as long as you're here."

"No, Eva."

"Yes, yes, as long as you're here!"

She looks forlorn and squeezes my hand all the time.

"No, Eva. Go! Never again!"

And nights go by and days come around. It's already three days since this conversation. Eva comes down the road with a load. How much wood this child has carried home from the forest this summer!

"Put down your load, Eva, and let me see if your eyes are just as blue as ever."

Her eyes were red.

"No, smile again, Eva! I won't resist you any longer, I'm yours, I'm yours. . . ."

Evening. Eva is singing; I can hear her song and a warmth runs through me.

"You're singing tonight, Eva?"

"Yes, I'm happy."

And since she's smaller than I, she jumps up a little to put her arms around my neck.

"But Eva, you've scratched your hands? Heavens, I wish you hadn't scratched them so!"

"It doesn't matter."

Her face is wonderfully radiant.

"Eva, have you talked to Mr. Mack?"

"Yes, once."

"What did he say, and what did you say?"

"He's become very hard on us, he makes my husband work night and day on the dock, and he also gives me all kinds of work to do. He's ordered me to do a man's job now."

"Why does he do that?"

Eva lowers her eyes.

"Why does he do it, Eva?"

"Because I love you."

"But how can he know that?"

"I told him."

Pause.

"I wish to God he weren't so hard on you, Eva!"

"But it doesn't matter. Nothing matters now."

And the sound of her voice in the forest was just like a little tremulous song.

And the leaves turn even more yellow, fall is approaching; more stars have appeared in the sky, and from now on the moon looks like a shadow of silver dipped in gold. There was no cold, nothing, just a cool stillness and a bustling life in the forest. Every tree stood there pondering. The berries were ripe.

Then came the twenty-second of August and the three Iron Nights.

XXVI

The first Iron Night.

The sun sets at nine. A faint darkness settles over the earth, a few stars can be seen, and two hours later there is a glimmer of moonlight. I wander into the woods with my gun and my dog; I build a fire, and the light from my fire shines in among the pine trunks. There's no frost.

The first Iron Night, I say. And I'm mysteriously thrilled by an intense, bewildering enjoyment of the particular time and place. . . .

A toast, ye men and beasts and birds, to the solitary night in the forest, in the forest. A toast to the darkness and to God's murmur among the trees, to the sweet, simple harmony of silence in my ears, to green leaves and yellow leaves! A toast to the sounds of life that I hear, a snuffling snout against the grass, a dog sniffing along the ground! A rousing toast to the wildcat with its throat on the ground and its eyes on the prey, preparing to spring on a sparrow in the dark, in the dark! A toast to the merciful stillness over the earth, to the stars and the crescent moon, yes, to it and to them! . . .

I stand up and listen. No one has heard me. I sit down again.

I give thanks for the solitary night, for the mountains, for the roar of the darkness and the sea that echoes in my own heart! I give thanks for my life, for my breath, for the grace of being alive tonight; for that I give thanks in my heart! Listen to the east and listen to the west, just listen! It's God eternal! The stillness murmuring in my ear is Nature's seething blood, God transfusing me and the world. I see a shiny gossamer thread in the light of my fire, I hear a rowboat moving in the harbor, while the aurora glides up the northern sky. And oh, how thankful I am, by my immortal soul, that it is I who am sitting here!

Quiet. A pine cone falls to the ground with a thud. A pine cone fell, I think to myself. The moon sits high in the sky, the flames flutter on the half-burned logs, about to go out. And I wander home late in the night.[31]

The second Iron Night, the same stillness and mild weather. My soul broods. Mechanically I go up to a tree, pull my cap over my forehead and lean my back against the tree, hands folded behind my neck. I stare and think, my eyes dazzled by the flames from my fire, though I don't feel it. I remain in this absurd position for a goodly while, gazing at the fire; my legs are the first to give out, getting stiff and tired, and I sit down. Only now do I consider what I have been doing. Why should I stare so long at the fire?

Aesop raises his head and listens, he hears footsteps. Eva appears among the trees.[32]

"I'm very preoccupied and sad tonight," I say.

And out of sympathy she makes no answer.

"I love three things," I then say. "I love a dream of love I once had, I love you, and I love this patch of earth."

"And which do you love best?"

"The dream."

Again there's quiet. Aesop knows Eva, he leans his head sideways and looks at her. I murmur, "I saw a girl on the road today, walking arm in arm with her lover. The girl pointed at me with her eyes and could barely keep from laughing as I passed."

"What was she laughing at?"

"I don't know. She must've laughed at me. Why do you ask?"

"Did you know her?"

"Yes. I bowed to her."

"And didn't she know you?"

"No, she pretended she didn't know me. . . .[33] But why do you sit here pumping me? It's mean of you. You won't hear her name from my lips."

Pause.

I murmur again, "What she was laughing at? She's a flirt; but what was she laughing at? For Christ's sake, what have I done to her?"

Eva answers, "It was mean of her to laugh at you—"

"No, it was not mean of her!" I scream. "You mustn't sit there and blame her, she never does anything mean, she was right to laugh at me. Shut up, damn it, and leave me alone, do you hear!"

And frightened, Eva leaves me alone. I look at her and instantly regret my harsh words; I throw myself down before her and wring my hands.

"Go home, Eva. It's you I love best; how could I love a dream? It was only a joke, it's you I love. But go home now, I'll come to you tomorrow. Remember I'm yours, yes, don't forget that. Good night."

And Eva goes home.

The third Iron Night, a night of the utmost suspense. If only there was a bit of frost! Instead of frost, a stagnant heat after the day's sun; the night was like a lukewarm morass. I kindled my fire. . . .

"Eva, there are times when it is a pleasure to be pulled by the hair. That's how warped a human mind can get. You are pulled by the hair up hill and down dale, and if someone asks what's going on, you answer in sheer ecstasy, I'm being pulled by the hair! And if they ask, But can't I help you, set you free? you answer, No. And if they ask, But can you stand it? you answer, Yes, I can stand it, because I love the hand that pulls me. . . . Do you know, Eva, what it is to hope?"

"Yes, I think so."

"You see, Eva, hope is a strange thing, yes, something very curious. You may be walking along some road one morning, hoping to meet someone you love there. And does the meeting come off? No. Why not? Because that someone is busy that morning and is in some other place altogether. . . . I once knew a blind old Lapp in the mountains. For fifty-eight years he hadn't seen a thing, and now he was past seventy. He felt he could see better and better as time went on, things were steadily looking up, he thought. Unless something untoward happened, he would be able to make out the sun in a few years. His hair was still black, but his eyes were quite white. When we sat smoking together in his turf hut, he told me about all the things he'd seen before he went blind. He was strong and hardy, without feeling, indestructible, and he kept up his hope. When I got ready to leave, he walked me out and began to point in different directions. 'There's the south,' he said, 'and there's the north. Now, go first in this direction, and when you get some way down the mountain you turn in that direction,' he said. 'Right you are!' I said. And then the Lapp laughed happily and said, 'Well, forty or fifty years ago I didn't know that, so I certainly see better now than I did then; things are getting better all the time.' Then he ducked and crept back into his turf hut, that perennial hut, his home on this earth. And he sat down before the fire again as usual, full of hope that in a few years he would be able to make out the sun. . . . Eva, it's a funny thing, hope is. For example, I'm right now hoping to forget the person I didn't meet on the road this morning."

"You speak so strangely."[34]

"It's the third Iron Night. I promise you, Eva, to be a different man tomorrow. Leave me to myself now. You won't recognize me tomorrow,[35] I'll laugh and kiss you, my own sweet girl. Just think, once this night is behind me I'll be a different man, in just a few hours. Good night, Eva."

"Good night."

I lie down closer to the fire to watch the flames. A spruce cone falls from a branch, a dry twig or two also drop to the ground. The night is like a bottomless gulf.[36] I close my eyes.

After an hour my senses begin to vibrate in a definite rhythm, I tune into the great stillness, I tune in. I gaze at the crescent moon sitting like a white shell in the sky, and I have a feeling of love for it, I feel I'm blushing. It's the moon, I say softly and passionately, it's the moon! And my heart beats toward it with a gentle throbbing. It lasts for several minutes. It blows a little, a strange wind is coming, an unusual blast of air. What is it? I look around and see no one. The wind calls me and my soul bows in answer to the call,[37] I feel myself lifted out of my sphere, pressed to an invisible breast, my eyes are moist with tears, I tremble—God is somewhere near looking at me. This lasts for another few minutes. I turn my head, the strange blast of air is gone, and I see something like the back of a spirit wandering soundlessly through the forest. . . .

I struggle briefly with a heavy stupor, worn out with emotion; I feel dead tired and fall asleep.

When I woke up the night was past. Alas, I had gone around in a sorry state for a long time, full of fever, waiting to collapse from some illness or other. Things had often turned topsy-turvy for me, I had seen everything with jaundiced eyes, possessed by a profound melancholy.

Now it was over.

XXVII

It's fall. The summer is gone, it vanished as quickly as it came. Ah, how quickly it went by! Now the days are cold, I hunt, fish and sing songs in the woods. And there are days when heavy fog comes floating in from the sea and envelops everything in darkness. On such a day something happened. I strayed in my wanderings into the forests of the parish-of-ease and emerged at the Doctor's house. There were visitors present, the young ladies I had met previously, young people dancing, regular crazy colts.

A carriage came rolling up and stopped by the garden gate; in the carriage sat Edvarda. She was taken aback when she saw me. "Goodbye!" I said quietly. But the Doctor detained me. At first Edvarda was made uncomfortable by my presence and lowered her eyes when I spoke; later she was better able to put up with me and even addressed a couple of brief questions to me. She was strikingly pale, the fog lay gray and cold on her face. She didn't alight from her carriage.

"I'm traveling on business," she said, laughing. "I've come from the parish church, where I couldn't find any of you; they told me you were here. I've been driving around for hours trying to find you. We're throwing a little party tomorrow night—in honor of the Baron, who is leaving next week—and I've been charged with inviting you all. There will be dancing too. Tomorrow night, remember."

Everybody bowed and thanked her.

To me she said further, "Please don't fail to come. Don't send a note at the last minute with excuses." She didn't say that to any of the others. Shortly afterward she drove off.

I was so touched by this unexpected kindness that I dropped out of sight for a moment to relish it. Then I took leave of the Doctor and his guests and headed for home. How gracious she was to me, how perfectly gracious! What could I do for her in return? My hands grew limp, a sweet chill flashed through my wrists. Dear me, I thought, here I go wobbly and faint with joy, unable to clench my fists and with tears in my eyes from helplessness! But what can be done about it? I got home only late in the evening. Going by way of the docks, I asked a fisherman if the packet boat would be there by tomorrow night. Oh no, the packet boat would only get in sometime next week. I rushed up to the hut and began to examine my best suit. I brushed it and made it nice; there were holes in it here and there, and I cried and mended the holes.

When I had finished I lay down on the bed. My rest lasts a mere moment; a thought occurs to me, I jump up and stand in the middle of the floor, shattered. The whole thing is just another trick! I whisper. I wouldn't have been invited if I hadn't chanced to be there when the others were invited. And what's more, she gave me the most obvious hint to stay away, to send a note with my excuses. . . .

I didn't sleep all night, and when morning came I took to the woods, frozen, exhausted from lack of sleep and feverish. Hey, they're preparing a party at Sirilund! So what? I'll neither go there nor send my excuses. Mr. Mack is a very thoughtful man, he's throwing this party for the Baron; but I won't show up, you understand? . . .

The fog lay thick over valleys and mountains, a clammy rime settled on my clothes and made them heavy, my face was cold and wet. There was only an occasional breath of wind, making the sleeping mists rise and fall, rise and fall.

It was well into the afternoon and getting dark. The fog hid everything from my eyes and I had no sun marks to go by. On my way home I wandered about for hours, but I was not in a rush; I wasn't very much bothered when I mistook the way, hitting upon unfamiliar places in the woods. Finally I place my gun against a tree and consult my compass. I plot my way exactly and start walking. It may be eight or nine o'clock.

Then something happened.

After half an hour I hear music through the fog, and a few minutes later I recognize the place—I'm close to the main building at Sirilund. Had my compass misled me to the very place I wanted to get away from? A familiar voice calls me, it's the Doctor's voice. Shortly afterward I'm led in.

Alas, maybe my gun barrel had influenced my compass and led it astray. I've had the same experience since, as recently as this year. I don't know what to think. Maybe it was fate.[38]

XXVIII

I had a bitter impression all evening that I shouldn't have come to this party. My arrival was hardly noticed, they were all so taken up with one another; Edvarda barely bid me welcome. I began drinking steadily because I realized I was not welcome, and yet I didn't leave.

Mr. Mack smiled a lot and showed his most agreeable

face, he was in evening dress and looked great. Now in one room, now in another, he mingled with the half-hundred guests, dancing a dance every now and then, joking and laughing. There were secrets lurking in his eyes.

A din of music and voices resounded throughout the house. Five of the rooms were occupied by the guests, besides the big parlor where they were dancing. By the time I arrived they had already had supper. Busy maids were running back and forth with glasses and wines, coffeepots of gleaming copper, cigars and pipes, cakes and fruit. Nothing was wanting. The chandeliers in the rooms were all set with extra-thick candles made for the occasion; the new oil lamps were lighted as well.

Eva was helping in the kitchen, I caught a glimpse of her. Imagine, Eva was here too![39]

The Baron received much attention, though he was quiet and modest and didn't push himself forward. He, too, was in evening dress, the tails of his coat were sadly crumpled from having been packed. He was constantly talking to Edvarda, followed her with his eyes, clinked glasses with her and called her "miss," as he did the daughters of the Dean and the district doctor. I felt a persistent antipathy for him and could barely glance at him without turning away with a pained and stupid grimace. When he spoke to me I replied curtly, whereupon I snapped my mouth shut.

I happen to remember a few things from that evening. Talking with a young girl, a blonde, I said something to her or told a story that made her laugh. It was scarcely a very remarkable story, but in my intoxicated condition I may have told it more amusingly than I can now remember; anyway, it has slipped my memory. Enough said. When I turned around, there was Edvarda standing behind me. She gave me an appreciative glance.

Later I noticed that she drew the blonde aside to learn what I had said. I cannot express how good that glance of Edvarda felt, after I had wandered about from room to room like an outcast all evening; I felt much more cheerful right away and afterward talked to a number of people and was quite amusing. As far as I know, I didn't commit any gaffes. . . .

I was standing out on the front steps. Then Eva appeared from one of the rooms carrying things. Seeing me, she came out onto the steps and quickly stroked my hands, whereupon she smiled and went in again. Neither of us had spoken. When I was about to follow her in, Edvarda stood in the hallway watching me. She looked straight at me. She didn't speak either. I went into the parlor.

"Just think, Lieutenant Glahn is amusing himself by having rendezvous with the servants out on the steps," Edvarda suddenly said in a loud voice. She was standing in the doorway. Several people heard what she said. She laughed as though she were joking, but her face was very pale.

I made no answer to this, I only mumbled, "It was by chance, she just came out and we met in the hallway. . . ."

Some time went by, perhaps an hour. A lady had a glass spilled over her dress. As soon as Edvarda saw this, she cried, "What's up? Of course, that's Glahn's doing."

I hadn't done it, I was standing in another part of the room when the accident occurred. From now on I drank rather steadily again, and kept near the door to be out of the way of the dancers.

The Baron was still gathering the ladies around him, he regretted that his collections had already been packed so that he couldn't display any of them: the cluster of seaweed from the White Sea, the clay from Korholmerne, exceedingly interesting mineral deposits from the seabed. The ladies peered inquisitively at his shirt studs, those five-pointed coronets that spelled Baron. Meanwhile the Doctor was a flop, even his witty oath, "by Jack and Jove," cut no ice anymore. But when Edvarda was speaking he was always at hand, again correcting her speech, driving her into a corner with his quibbles, keeping her down with calm superiority.

She said, ". . . until I cross the valley of death."

"Cross what?" the Doctor asked.

"The valley of death. Isn't that what it's called, the valley of death?"

"I've heard people talk about the river of death. I believe that's what you mean."

Later she spoke about guarding something like a—

"Dragon," the Doctor cut in.

"All right. Like a dragon," she replied.

But the Doctor said, "Now, thank me for bailing you out. I'm sure you meant to say 'Argus'."

The Baron raised his eyebrows and gave him a surprised look through his thick glasses. He had probably never heard such corny jokes before. But the Doctor didn't turn a hair. A lot he cared about the Baron!

I'm still standing by the door. In the parlor the dancing goes swimmingly. I manage to get a conversation going with the governess from the parsonage. We talked about the war, about the conditions in the Crimea, the events in France, Napoleon as emperor and his protection of the Turks; the young lady had read the papers during the summer and could report the news to me. Finally we sit down on a sofa to talk.

Then Edvarda comes by, stopping in front of us. Suddenly she says, "You must pardon me, Lieutenant, for surprising you on the steps. I'll never do it again, Sir."

And once more she laughed, but she didn't look at me.

"Miss Edvarda, why don't you stop it!" I said.

She had called me "Sir," which boded no good, and she had a malicious expression on her face. I thought of the Doctor and cavalierly shrugged my shoulders, as he would have done. She said, "But why don't you go out into the kitchen, Sir? Eva is there. I think you should stay out there."

She followed this up with a baleful glance.

I hadn't been to very many parties, but I had never heard a

tone like that at the few I had attended.[40] I said, "Aren't you running the risk of being misunderstood, Miss Edvarda?"

"No, how's that? Well, perhaps, but how?"

"You speak so hastily at times. Just now, for example, it seemed to me you positively banished me to the kitchen, and that of course would be a misunderstanding. After all, I know very well you didn't mean to be rude."

She walks a few steps away from us. I could tell by her face that she was all along pondering what I had said. Turning around, she comes back and says breathlessly, "It was no misunderstanding, Lieutenant, you heard me correctly, Sir, I banished you to the kitchen."

"Oh, but Edvarda!" exclaimed the horrified governess.

And I began once more to talk about the war and the conditions in the Crimea; but my thoughts were far away from there. I was no longer intoxicated, only quite dazed; the ground was slipping from under my feet and once more, as on so many another unhappy occasion, I was thrown off balance. I get up from the sofa and want to go out. I'm stopped by the Doctor.

"I've just now been listening to a eulogy of you," he says.

"A eulogy? From whom?"

"From Edvarda. She's still standing over there in the corner gazing ardently at you. I shall never forget it, she looked absolutely in love judging by her eyes, and she said out loud how much she admired you."

"That's nice," I replied with a laugh. Alas, there wasn't a clear thought in my head.

I went up to the Baron, bent over him as if I wanted to whisper something to him, and when I was close enough I spit in his ear. He jumped up and greeted my behavior with an idiotic stare. Later I noticed that he related the incident to Edvarda and that she was annoyed. She was probably[41] thinking of the shoe I had thrown into the water, of the cups and glasses I had had the misfortune to break, and all the other infractions of good form I had committed. It was bound to be revived in her memory again, every bit of it. I felt ashamed, it was all over with me; wherever I turned I met frightened and astonished looks, and I stole away from Sirilund without a word of goodbye or thanks.

XXIX

The Baron is leaving. All right, I'll load my gun, take to the mountains and fire a loud shot in his and Edvarda's honor. I'll drill a deep hole in a cliff and blow up a mountain in his and Edvarda's honor. And a big rock will roll down the mountainside and crash mightily into the sea as his ship passes by. I know a place, a break in the mountain, where rocks have rolled before and made a clear path all the way to the sea. Far below there is a boat landing.

"Two drills!" I say to the blacksmith.

And the blacksmith sharpens two drills. . . .

Eva has been set to driving back and forth between the mill and the pier with one of Mr. Mack's horses. She has to do a man's job and transport sacks of grain and flour. I meet her—she looks marvelous with her fresh face. Good God, how tenderly her smile glows. I met her every evening.

"You look as if you don't have a worry in the world, Eva, my love."

"You call me your love! I'm an uneducated woman, but I'll be true to you. I'll be true to you even if I have to die for it. Mr. Mack is getting stricter every day, but I think nothing of it; he rants and raves, but I don't answer him. He grabbed my arm and turned gray with rage. I have only *one* worry."

"And what worry is that?"

"Mr. Mack is threatening you. He says to me, 'Aha, you've got that Lieutenant on the brain!' I reply, 'Yes, I belong to him.' Then he says, 'Just you wait, I'll soon get rid of him, you bet!' He said that yesterday."

"It doesn't matter, let him threaten. . . . Eva, may I see if your feet are as tiny as ever? Shut your eyes and let me see!"

And, with her eyes shut, she throws her arms about my neck. A tremor passes through her. I carry her into the woods. The horse stands and waits.[42]

XXX

I'm up in the mountains drilling. The fall air is crystal-clear all around. The blows on my drill ring steady and rhythmical, Aesop watches me with wondering eyes. Every now and then an onrush of satisfaction courses through my breast; nobody knows that I'm here in the lonely mountains.

The birds of passage are gone—a pleasant journey and welcome back! Willow tits, along with other tits and an occasional hedge-sparrow, now live alone on the rock-strewn slopes and in the thickets: peep-peep! Everything is so strangely changed —the dwarf birch bleeds red against the gray rocks, a bluebell here and a willow herb there rise out of the heather, swaying and gently humming a song: hssh! But above it all there hovers an osprey with outstretched neck, heading deeper into the mountains.

Evening comes, and I put away my drills and my mallet under a rock and take a rest. Everything slumbers, the moon glides up in the north, the cliffs cast gigantic shadows. There is a full moon, it looks like a glowing island, like a round mystery of brass that I skirt and wonder at. Aesop gets up and is restless.

What do you want, Aesop? As for me, I'm tired of my grief, I want to forget it, drown it. I order you to lie still, Aesop, I

won't have any noise. Eva asks, Do you think of me sometimes? I answer, Of you, always. Eva asks again, And does it
give you joy to think of me? I answer, Sheer joy, never anything but joy. Then Eva says, Your hair is turning gray. And I
answer, Yes, it's beginning to turn gray. But Eva asks, Is it
turning gray because of something you're thinking? And to that
I answer, Maybe. At last Eva says, Then you aren't thinking
only of me. . . . Aesop, lie still, I'd rather tell you something
else. . . .

But Aesop stands sniffing excitedly down at the valley, whining and tugging at my clothes. When I finally get up and follow
him, he can't get away fast enough. A red glow shows in the
sky over the forest, I press on, a fire appears before my eyes, a
huge bonfire. I stop and stare, walk a few steps and stare
again—my hut is in flames.

XXXI

The fire was the work of Mr. Mack, I saw through it from the
very first. I lost my skins and my bird's wings, I lost my stuffed
eagle; everything burned. What now? I lay under the open sky
for two nights without going to Sirilund to ask for shelter;
finally I rented an abandoned fisherman's cabin near the docks
and caulked it with dried moss. I slept on a cartload of red
bearberry heather from the mountains. I was once more home
free.

Edvarda sent a message to say that she had heard about my
misfortune and offered me, on her father's behalf, a room at
Sirilund. Edvarda touched? Edvarda magnanimous? I sent no
answer. Thank God, I was no longer without shelter, and it
made me feel both pride and joy to ignore Edvarda's offer. I
met her on the road with the Baron, they were walking arm

in arm; I looked them both squarely in the eye and bowed in passing. She stopped and asked, "So you won't come and stay with us, Lieutenant?"

"I've already prepared my new place," I answered, stopping also.

She looked at me, her breast heaving.

"You wouldn't have suffered any harm with us either," she said.

My heart was stirred to gratitude, but I couldn't bring myself to say anything.

The Baron slowly walked on.

"Perhaps you don't want to see me anymore?" she asks.

"I thank you, Miss Edvarda, for offering me a roof over my head when my hut burned down," I said. "It was all the nobler of you since it was scarcely done with your father's consent." And I thanked her with bared head for her offer.

"In God's name, don't you ever want to see me again, Glahn?" she said suddenly.

The Baron called.

"The Baron is calling," I said, again removing my cap and making a deep bow.

And I wandered up into the mountains to my blasting site. Nothing, nothing would ever again shake my composure. I met Eva. "There, you see!" I cried. "Mr. Mack cannot drive me away. He burned my hut down, and already I've got another hut. . . ." She was carrying a brush and a tar bucket. "What now, Eva?"

Mr. Mack had turned over a boat at the landing under the cliff and ordered her to tar it. He watched her every step, she had to obey.

"But why exactly at the landing? Why not on the dock?"

Mr. Mack had given the order, so—

"Eva, Eva, my love, you've been turned into a slave and you don't complain. Look, now you're smiling again, and life sparkles in your smile though you are a slave."

When I came to my blasting hole, I was met by a surprise. I noticed that somebody had been there, I examined the tracks in the gravel and recognized the imprints of Mr. Mack's long, pointed shoes. What is he nosing about here for? I thought to myself, giving a look around. Nobody could be seen. My suspicion was not aroused.

And I started hammering on my drill without the faintest idea of what harm I was doing.

XXXII

The packet boat arrived, bringing me my uniform; it was to take the Baron and all his crates of shells and seaweed varieties on board. It was now loading barrels of herring and cod-liver oil at the pier; it would be leaving toward evening.

I grab my gun and load both barrels with plenty of powder. Having done so, I nodded to myself. I go up into the mountains and fill my blasting hole with powder as well; again I nod. Now all was ready. I lay down to wait.

I waited for hours. All along I could hear the steamer's capstan hoisting and lowering stuff at the pier. It was already getting dark. Finally the whistle blows, the cargo is on board, the ship leaves. Now I have a few minutes of waiting. The moon was not up, and I stared like crazy through the evening dusk.

As soon as the foremost point of the bow emerged from behind the islet, I lighted my fuse and swiftly withdrew. A minute goes by. Suddenly there is a bang, a spray of rock fragments shoots up into the air, the mountain shakes, and the rock goes crashing into the abyss. The echo reverberates from the cliffs round about. I grab my gun and fire one barrel; the echo answers many times over. After a moment I also fire the second barrel. My salute made the air tremble, and the echo flung the

din out into the wide world; it was as though the mountains
all around had banded together to salute the departing ship with
a mighty shout. A few moments pass, the air quiets down, the
echo falls silent among the cliffs, and the earth lies still once
again. The ship disappears in the twilight.

I'm still trembling with a mysterious excitement, I take my
drills and my gun under my arm and, wobbly at the knees, set
off down the mountainside. I take the shortest way, keeping
an eye on the smoking track left by my avalanche. Aesop keeps
shaking his head all the time and sneezes at the smell of
burning.

When I got down to the boat landing, I was met by a sight
that plunged me into the most violent agitation: lying there
was a boat, crushed by the fallen rock, and Eva—Eva lay beside
it, smashed to bits, split open by a blow, her side and abdomen
cut up beyond recognition. Eva had died instantaneously.

XXXIII

What more is there for me to write? I didn't fire a shot for
several days, I had no food, nor did I eat anything; I sat in my
shack. Eva was taken to the church in Mr. Mack's white-
painted houseboat, I went overland and showed up at the
graveside.

Eva is dead. Do you remember her little girlish head with
hair like a nun's? She came so quietly, put down her load and
smiled. And did you see how that smile sparkled with life? Shut
up, Aesop! I remember a strange legend from four generations
back, in Iselin's time, when Stamer was parson.

A maiden was imprisoned in a stone tower. She loved a lord.
Why? Ask the wind and the stars, ask the god of life; for no
one else knows these things. And the lord was her friend and

her lover; but time passed, and one fine day he saw someone else and his heart turned away.

As a youth he loved the maiden. Often he called her his bliss and his dove, and her embrace was hot and heaving. He said, Give me your heart! And she did so. He said, May I ask you for something, my love? And she answered, in raptures, Yes. She gave him all, and yet he never thanked her.

The other one he loved like a slave, like a madman and a beggar. Why? Ask the dust on the road and the falling leaves, ask life's mysterious god; for no one else knows these things. She gave him nothing, no, nothing did she give him, and yet he thanked her. She said, Give me your peace and your sanity. And he only grieved that she didn't ask for his life.

And the maiden was put in the tower. . . .

What are you doing, maiden, you're smiling?

I'm thinking of something from ten years ago. That was when I met him.

You remember him still?

I remember him still.

And time passes. . . .

What are you doing, maiden? And why are you smiling?

I'm sewing his name on his table linen.

Whose name? Of him who shut you up?

Yes, of him I met twenty years ago.

You remember him still?

I remember him the same as ever.

And time passes. . . .

What are you doing, prisoner?

I'm growing old and can no longer see to sew, I scrape the plaster from the wall. From the plaster I'll form a jar, as a small present to him.

Of whom are you speaking?

Of my lover, of him who shut me up in the tower.

He shut you up and you smile at it?

I'm wondering what he will say now. Look, look, he will

say, my sweetheart has sent me a little jar, she hasn't forgotten me after thirty years.

And time passes. . . .

What, prisoner! You're doing nothing and you smile?

I'm growing old, growing old, my eyes are blind, I do nothing but think.

Of him that you met forty years ago?

Of him that I met when I was young. Maybe it was forty years ago.

But don't you know that he's dead? You turn pale, old one, you do not answer, your lips are white, you don't breathe anymore. . . .

Well, thus went the strange legend of the maiden in the tower. Wait a little, Aesop, I forgot something: one day she heard her lover's voice in the courtyard and she fell on her knees and blushed. She was then forty years old. . . .

I bury you, Eva, and humbly kiss the sand on your grave. A rich, roseate memory glides through my heart when I think of you, it's as though I'm showered with blessings when I remember your smile. You gave all, your very all, and it cost you no effort, for you were the exuberant child of life itself. Yet others, who are chary even of their glances, may possess all my thoughts. Why? Ask the twelve months and the ships in the sea, ask the mysterious god of the heart. . . .

XXXIV

A man said, "You don't shoot anymore? Aesop is baying in the woods, he's chasing a hare."

I said, "Go and shoot it for me."

A few days went by. Mr. Mack paid me a visit, looking

hollow-eyed, his face gray. I thought, Is it true that I can see through people or isn't it? I don't really know.

Mr. Mack spoke about the rockfall, the disaster. It was an accident, a tragic coincidence. I was in no way to blame.

I said, "If there was someone who wanted to separate Eva and me at any cost, he has achieved his purpose. God damn him!"

Mr. Mack squinted suspiciously at me. He mumbled something about a lovely funeral. No expense had been spared.

I sat there admiring his great adroitness.

He didn't want any compensation for the boat that my avalanche had crushed.

"But no!" I said. "You really won't charge me for the boat and the tar bucket, and the brush?"

"Why, my good Lieutenant!" he replied. "How can you think such a thing!" And he looked at me with eyes full of hatred.

I didn't see Edvarda for three weeks. Well, once, when I met her at the store where I'd gone to buy a loaf of bread; she stood behind the counter rummaging through various materials. Besides her, only the two clerks were present.

I said a loud hello, and she looked up but didn't answer. It occurred to me that I wouldn't ask for bread in her presence, so I turned to the clerks and asked for buckshot and powder. I kept an eye on her while these articles were weighed.

A gray, much too small dress with frayed buttonholes; her flat breast heaved intensely. How she had grown during the summer! Her forehead was thoughtful, those unusual arched eyebrows were like two riddles in her face, all her movements had become more mature. I looked at her hands—the expression of those long, delicate fingers affected me powerfully and made me tremble. She was still rummaging among the fabrics.

I stood there wishing that Aesop would slip behind the

counter, run up and recognize her, then I could immediately call him back and apologize. What would she have answered?

"There you are!" says the clerk.

I paid, picked up my parcels and bid her goodbye. She looked up, but again didn't answer. Good! I thought; she may be the Baron's bride already. And I left without my loaf of bread.

When I got outside I glanced up at the window. Nobody's eyes were following me.

XXXV

Then one night the snow came and it began to feel chilly in my hut. There was a fireplace where I cooked my food, but the wood burned poorly and the walls were very drafty, though I had caulked them as well as I could. Fall was past and the days were growing short. The first snow still melted in the sun, leaving the ground bare again, but the nights were cold and the water froze. And all the grass and all the insects died.

A mysterious stillness settled on the people, they brooded and were silent, their eyes awaiting the winter. No shouts were heard from the drying grounds anymore and the harbor was quiet; everything was getting ready for the endless auroral night when the sun slept in the sea. From a solitary boat came the muffled sounds of the oars.

A girl came rowing.

"Where have you been, my lass?"

"Nowhere."

"Nowhere? Come, I know you, we met last summer."

She came alongside, stepped ashore and made the boat fast.

"You were a shepherd girl, you were knitting a stocking. We met one night."

A faint blush mantles her cheeks and she laughs bashfully.

"My little highland lass, come into the hut and let me look at you. Come to think of it, your name is Henriette."

But she walks past me without a word. Fall, winter had taken hold of her, her senses were asleep.

Already the sun had dipped into the sea.

XXXVI

And for the first time I put on my uniform and went down to Sirilund. My heart was pounding.

I remembered everything from that first day when Edvarda came rushing up to me and embraced me in front of everybody; now she had tossed me hither and thither for months, making my hair turn gray. My own fault? Yes, my star had led me astray. I thought, How she will gloat if I throw myself at her feet today and tell her my heart's secret! She will offer me a chair and call for some wine, and as she raises the glass to her lips to drink with me she will say, Thank you, Lieutenant, for the time we've spent together, I'll never forget it! But if I then feel glad and show a little hope, she will only pretend to drink and put her glass down untouched. And she won't hide from me that she merely pretends to drink, that's the very thing she wants me to see. It's her way.

Well and good! Before long the final hour will strike.

And as I went down the road I thought further, My uniform will impress her, its braids are new and handsome. My officer's sword will clatter against the floor. A nervous joy thrilled through me and I whispered to myself, Who knows what may happen yet? I raised my head and brandished my arm. No more humility now, have a spark of honor! I didn't care what hap-

pened, I would make no more overtures. Pardon me, fair
maiden, that I do not ask for your hand. . . .

Mr. Mack met me in the yard, grayer and still more hollow-
eyed.

"Leaving? You don't say. Well, you probably haven't had a
very pleasant time lately, eh? Your hut was burned down."
And Mr. Mack smiled.

Suddenly I felt as if I were seeing the world's smartest man
in front of me.

"Go in, Lieutenant, Edvarda is inside. Well, goodbye. Anyway, we'll probably see each other at the pier when the ship
sails." He walked away, head bowed, thoughtful, whistling.

Edvarda sat in the parlor reading. When I stepped in, she
was momentarily surprised at my uniform; she gave me a side-
long look, like a bird, and even blushed. Her mouth fell open.

"I've come to say goodbye," I finally managed to say.

She got up at once, and I could see that my words had made
an impact on her.

"Glahn, you're leaving? Now?"

"As soon as the ship comes." I grasp her hand, both her
hands, a senseless rapture takes possession of me, and I exclaim,
"Edvarda!" and stare at her.

And in the same moment she's cold, cold and defiant. She
resisted me with all she had, she drew herself up. I felt like a
beggar before her, released her hands and let her go. From that
moment on, I remember, I kept repeating mechanically, "Edvarda! Edvarda!" several times without thinking, and when she
asked, "Yes? What were you going to say?" I didn't give a
word of explanation.

"To think that you're leaving already!" she said again. "Who
will be coming next year?"

"Someone else," I replied. "I suppose the hut will be rebuilt."

Pause. She was already reaching for her book.

"I'm sorry my father is not around," she said. "But I'll pass
your regards on to him."

To this I made no answer. I stepped forward, took her hand once more and said, "Well, goodbye, Edvarda."

"Goodbye," she answered.

I opened the door as if to go. Already she sat with the book in her hand, reading, really reading and turning the pages. My departure had made no impression on her, none at all.

I coughed.

She turned around and said, surprised, "Oh, you haven't left? I thought you had left."

God only knows, but her surprise was too great; forgetting to be on guard, she exaggerated her surprise, and it occurred to me that perhaps she had known all along that I was standing behind her.

"Now I'm leaving," I said.

Then she got up and came over to me.

"I would like to have a remembrance of you, now that you're going away," she said. "I had meant to ask you for something, but I suppose it's too much. Will you give me Aesop?"

Without giving it any thought, I replied "Yes."

"Then perhaps you could bring it tomorrow?" she said.

I left.

I looked up at the window. No one there.

It was all over. . . .

The last night in the hut. I brooded, counting the hours; when the morning came I prepared my last meal. It was a cold day.

Why did she ask me to bring the dog to her myself? Did she want to talk to me, tell me something for the last time? I had nothing more to hope for. And how would she treat Aesop? Aesop, Aesop, she will torture you! For my sake, she will whip you, pet you too perhaps, but certainly whip you in and out of season and completely ruin you. . . .

I called Aesop, patted him, put our heads together and grabbed my gun. He was already whining for joy, thinking we were going hunting. Again I put our heads together, placed the muzzle of my gun against Aesop's neck and fired.

I hired a man to bring Aesop's body to Edvarda.

XXXVII

The packet boat was to depart in the afternoon.

I went down to the pier, my luggage was already on board. Mr. Mack shook my hand and cheered me by saying I would have nice weather, pleasant weather, he wouldn't mind taking a trip himself in such weather. Then the Doctor came, along with Edvarda; I felt my knees beginning to tremble.

"We wanted to see you well on board," the Doctor said.

I thanked him.

Edvarda looked me straight in the eye and said, "I'm much obliged to you, Sir, for giving me your dog." She pinched her mouth, her lips were white. Again she had called me "Sir."

"When will the ship be leaving?" the Doctor asked some man.

"In half an hour."

I said nothing.

Agitated, Edvarda was turning hither and thither.

"Doctor, shouldn't we go home again?" she asked. "I have done that which was my errand."

"You have accomplished your errand," the Doctor said.

She laughed, humiliated by his perpetual corrections, and replied, "Yes, wasn't that just about what I said?"

"No," he answered shortly.

I looked at him. The little man stood there, cold and solid; he had made a plan and was following it to the finish. And what if he lost despite everything? Even so, he wouldn't show it, he never moved a muscle in his face.

It was getting dark.

"Well, goodbye," I said. "And thanks for every single day."

Edvarda looked at me without a word. Then she turned her head and stood looking out at the ship.

I got into the boat. Edvarda was still standing on the pier. After I had boarded, the Doctor called goodbye. I looked ashore. At that very moment Edvarda turned and left the pier to go home, hastily and with the Doctor far behind her. That was the last I saw of her.

A wave of sadness swept through my heart. . . .

The steamer started off; I could still see Mr. Mack's sign: SALT AND BARRELS IN STOCK. But soon it was blotted out. The moon and the stars came out, the mountains rose round about, and I could see the endless forests. There is the mill, there—there lay the hut that was burned down; the tall gray rock is left all by itself on the site of the fire. Iselin, Eva . . .

The auroral night spreads over hills and dales.

XXXVIII

I have written this to while away the time. It amused me to think back to that summer in Nordland, when I often counted the hours and yet time flew. Everything is changed, the days won't slip by anymore.

I still enjoy many a merry hour, but time stands still, and I don't understand why it should stand so still. I've left the service and am free as a king, all is well, I meet people and ride in carriages. Now and then I close one eye and write with my forefinger on the sky; I tickle the moon under the chin and seem to catch it laughing, laughing uproariously with foolish glee at being tickled under the chin. Everything smiles. I pop a cork and bring together merry people.

As for Edvarda, I do not think of her. Why shouldn't I have
forgotten her altogether after all this time? I do, after all, have
a sense of honor. And if anyone asks me whether I have any
regrets, I answer with a flat no—that I have no regrets. . . .

Cora is looking at me. Before it was Aesop, but now it's
Cora that lies there looking at me.[43] The clock ticks on the
mantelpiece, the hubbub of the city rumbles outside my open
windows. There is a knock at the door and the postman hands
me a letter. The letter has a coronet on it. I know who it is
from; I understand immediately, or maybe I dreamed it some
sleepless night. But there's nothing written in the letter, it contains only two green bird's feathers.

A freezing terror runs through me, I turn cold. Two green
feathers! I say to myself. Well, what is to be done about it! But
why am I turning cold? Come, there's a damn draft from those
windows over there!

And I shut the windows.

Well, there they lie, two bird's feathers! I go on thinking; I
feel I ought to know them, they remind me of a little joke up
in Nordland, one of those little adventures among many others.
It was amusing to see those two feathers again. And suddenly
I seem to see a face and hear a voice, and the voice says,
"Please, Lieutenant, here are your feathers, Sir!"

Your feathers, *Sir!* . . .

Cora, lie still, do you hear, if you don't I'll kill you! The
weather is warm, it's unbearably hot; what was I thinking of
when I shut the windows! Open the windows again, open the
door wide, come hither, ye merry people, come in! Hey, por-
ter, run an errand for me, go and hunt up lots of people. . . .[44]

And the day goes by, but time stands still.[45]

I've written this purely for my own amusement, enjoying myself as best I could. I'm not weighed down by grief, I just long
to go away, whereto I don't know, but far away, maybe to
Africa, or to India. For I belong to the forest and to solitude.

GLAHN'S DEATH

A Document from 1861

I

The Glahn family may still go on advertising in the papers for the lost Lieutenant Thomas Glahn for a long time; but he will never come back anymore. He is dead, and I even know how he died.

If it comes to that, I am not at all surprised that his family still persists in its inquiries; for Thomas Glahn was in many ways an exceptional and lovable man. In fairness to him I must admit this, despite the fact that Glahn is still repugnant to my soul and his memory arouses my hatred. He looked gorgeous, was bursting with youth and had a seductive manner. When he looked at you with his hot animal eyes you clearly felt his power, even I felt it. A woman is supposed to have said, "When he looks at me I am lost; it produces an excitement in me, as if he touched me."

But Thomas Glahn had his faults, and I do not intend to gloss over them, since I hate him. At times he could be silly as a child, so good-natured was he; perhaps that was why he charmed the females as he did, God only knows. He would jabber with the women and laugh at their inane twaddle, and this way he made an impression on them. Once he said about a very corpulent man in town that he looked as if he had grease in his pants, and then he laughed at his own crack, whereas I would have felt ashamed of it. Later, after we had come to live together in the same house, he once showed his silliness in a blatant way: one morning my landlady came to my room and asked what I wanted for breakfast, and offhand I happened to answer, "A bread and a slice of egg." Thomas Glahn, who was sitting in my room right then—he was staying in the attic up above, directly under the roof—started laughing like a child at my trifling slip of the tongue and to gloat over it. "A bread and a slice of egg!" he kept repeating endlessly, until I looked at him in surprise and made him stop.

111

Later perhaps I will remember more of his ridiculous traits, in which case I will write them down, too, and not spare him, since he is still my enemy. Why should I be magnanimous? I must admit, though, that he blathered only when he was drunk. But is not being drunk a great fault in itself?

When I met him in the fall of 1859, he was a man of thirty-two, we were both the same age. At that time he had a full beard and wore woolen hunting shirts with excessively low necklines; even so he sometimes neglected closing the top button. At first his neck struck me as being exceptionally beautiful, but little by little he turned me into his mortal enemy, and then I thought his neck was no better-looking than my own, though I didn't make such a big show of it. I met him the first time on a river boat, bound for the same place as he to hunt, and we decided at once to go upcountry by oxcart together when the railroad couldn't take us any farther. I purposely omit giving the name of the place where we were going, so as not to put anyone on the trail; but the Glahn family can safely stop advertising for their relation, because he lies dead in the place we traveled to and that I forbear mentioning by name.

I had heard of Thomas Glahn before I met him, by the way, his name was not unknown to me. I'd heard he had had an affair with a young Nordland woman from a big house and that he had compromised her somehow or other, whereupon she had sent him packing. In his foolish defiance, he had then sworn to revenge this on himself, and the lady calmly let him do as he pleased in that regard, it was no concern of hers. Only from now on did Thomas Glahn's name become really well known; he cut loose, went crazy, drank, caused one scandal after another and resigned his commission. What an odd way of revenging yourself for being jilted!

There was also another story going around touching his relationship with the young lady: that he had by no means compromised her but that her family had thrown him out, and that she herself had helped them do so after a Swedish count, whose name I shall not mention, had asked for her hand. But this report I put less trust in, regarding the first as the truer one; after all, I hate Thomas Glahn and believe him capable of the worst. But whatever the case may have been, he never himself spoke about this affair with the high-ranking lady, nor did I ask him about it. What business was it of mine?

As we sat there on the river boat, I don't recall talking about anything else but the little village we were bound for and where neither of us had been before.

"It's supposed to have a sort of hotel," Glahn said, consulting the map. "If we're lucky we may get to stay there; the landlady is an old English half-breed, I've been told. The headman lives in the neighboring village, he's said to have many wives, some no more than ten years old."

Well, I had no idea whether or not the headman had many wives, or whether there was a hotel in the village, so I said nothing; but Glahn smiled, and I thought his smile was beautiful.

I forgot to mention, incidentally, that he could by no means be called a perfect man, though he looked so gorgeous. He told me himself that he had an old gunshot wound in his left foot and that this wound grew acutely rheumatic at any change in the weather.

II

A week later we were put up in the large hut that they called the hotel, with the old English half-breed. Ah, what a hotel! The walls were of clay and a bit of wood, and the wood had been chewed through by the white ants that crawled about everywhere. I lived in a room next to the parlor, with a green glass window facing the street, one single pane that was not very clean, and Glahn had chosen a tiny little hole up in the attic, where he also had a single pane facing the street but where it was much darker and less livable. The sun beat down on the thatched roof and made his room almost unbearably hot night and day; moreover, far from there being a stairway up to his place, there was only a miserable ladder with four steps. What could I do about it? Leaving Glahn to choose, I said, "There are two rooms, one downstairs and one upstairs, take your pick!"

And Glahn looked the two rooms over and took the room at the top, perhaps to give me the better one; but didn't I also show my gratitude to him for that? I owe him nothing.

As long as the heat was at its worst, we refrained from hunting and stayed quietly around the hut; for the heat was extremely severe. We lay with a fly-net around the bed at night on account of the insects, but even so blind bats would sometimes come flying noiselessly, hit the nets at full blast and tear them to pieces. This happened all too often to Glahn, because he had to keep a hatch in the roof open all the time because of the heat, but it did not happen to me. During the day we would lie on mats in front of our hut, smoking and observing life around the other huts. The natives were brown, thick-lipped people, all with rings in their ears and dead brown eyes; they were almost naked, with nothing but a strip of cotton fabric or a braid made of leaves around their loins, and the women had also a short cotton skirt to cover themselves with. All the children were stark naked day and night, with big, protruding bellies that glistened with oil.

"The women are too fat," Glahn said.

And I too thought the women were too fat, and it may not have been Glahn but I myself who first thought so; but I won't argue the point and gladly give him the credit. Besides, not all the women were ugly, though their faces were fat and puffy; I had met a girl in the village, a young Tamil half-caste with long hair and snow-white teeth, she was the prettiest of them all. I ran across her one evening on the edge of a rice paddy, she was lying flat on her stomach in the tall grass kicking her legs in the air. She could talk to me, and so we talked together as long as I liked; it was nearly morning before we parted, and then she did not go straight home but feigned having spent the night in the neighboring village. That evening, Glahn was sitting outside a little hut in the middle of the village with two other girls who were very young, perhaps no more than ten years old. There he sat flirting and drinking rice beer with them, that was what he fancied.

A few days later we went out hunting. We passed tea gardens, rice paddies and grassy plains, leaving the village behind us and going in the direction of the river; we came into forests of strange foreign trees, bamboo and mango, tamarind, teak and salt trees, oil and rubber plants—God knows what sort of trees they all were, neither of us understood very much about it. But there was little water in the river, and it continued that way until the rainy season. We shot wild pigeons and partridges, and in the afternoon we saw two panthers; overhead parrots were flying about. Glahn was a crack shot, he never missed; but that was really because his gun was better than mine, I was also a crack shot quite often. I never boasted of it, but Glahn would often say, "I'll stab that one in the tail," or "I'll scratch the head of that one." He would say these things before pulling the trigger, and when the bird dropped to the ground, sure enough, he had hit it in the tail or in the head. When we ran across the two panthers, Glahn insisted on attacking them, too, with his shotgun; but I made him forget about it, it was getting dark and we had only a couple of cartridges left. He also put on airs about this—that he had shown himself courageous enough to attack panthers with a shotgun.

"It bothers me that I didn't shoot after all," he said to me. "Why are you so damn cautious? Do you want to live to be old?"

"I'm glad you find me more reasonable than yourself," I replied.

"Well, let's not quarrel over trifles," he then said.

Those were his words and not mine; if he had wanted to pick a quarrel, OK by me. I was beginning to dislike him for his frivolous behavior and his seductive ways. Only the night before I had been quietly walking along with my friend Maggie, the Tamil girl, and we were both in high spirits. And there sits Glahn in front of the hut, nodding and smiling to us as we walk past; Maggie, who saw him for the first time then, became curious and pumped me for information about him. So much of an impression had he made on her that, when we parted and went our separate ways, she did not come home with me.

Glahn wanted to make light of it, as if it were of no importance, when I spoke to him about it. But I didn't forget it. Nor was it to me he had laughed and smiled as we walked past the hut, it was to Maggie.

"What is she chewing all the time?" he asked me.

"I don't know," I replied. "She's just chewing, that's what she's got teeth for, I suppose."

It was no news to me either that Maggie was constantly chewing something, I had been noticing that for a long time. But it was not betel she chewed, for her teeth were perfectly white; rather, she was in the habit of chewing all sorts of other things, sticking them in her mouth and chewing them as though they were sweets. It could be anything whatever, coins, bits of paper, feathers, she chewed it all. Still, this was no reason to disparage her, since she was the prettiest girl in the village in spite of it; but Glahn was envious of me, that was the crux of the matter.

Anyway, the next evening I made it up again with Maggie, and we didn't see anything of Glahn.

III

A week passed, we went hunting every day and shot a lot of game. One morning, just as we were entering the forest, Glahn grabbed my arm and whispered, "Stop!" The same instant he smacks the rifle to his cheek and fires. It was a young leopard that he shot. I could also have fired then, but Glahn kept that honor for himself and fired first. How this will make him brag again! I thought. We walked up to the dead animal—it was stone-dead, its left flank ripped open, and the bullet was embedded in its back.

I'm not fond of being grabbed by the arm, so I said, "I could also have managed that shot."

Glahn looked at me.

I say again, "Perhaps you don't think I could have done it?"

Still Glahn does not answer. Instead he continues to show his childishness and shoots the dead leopard again, this time through the head. I look at him, thunderstruck.

"Well," he goes on to explain, "I can't let anyone know I hit a leopard in the flank."[46]

It was more than his vanity could take to have been such a poor shot, he always wanted to be first. What vanity! But it was none of my business, I was not going to give him away.

When we got back to the village with the dead leopard that evening, many of the natives turned out to view it. However, Glahn merely said that we had shot it in the morning and didn't make too much of a show of it. Maggie also turned up.

"Who shot it?" she asked.

"You can see that, can't you? Two wounds—we shot it this morning when we went out." And he turned the animal over and showed her the two bullet wounds, both the one in the flank and the one in the head. "This is where my bullet went in," he said, pointing at the wound in the flank, wanting in his vanity to let me take credit for hitting it in the head. I couldn't be bothered to correct him, nor did I do so. Then Glahn began to treat the natives to rice beer, giving out lots of it to any who cared to drink.

"You both shot it," Maggie said to herself; yet she was all the time looking at Glahn.

I pulled her aside and said, "Why are you looking at him all the time? I'm here, too, am I not?"

"Sure," she replied. "And listen, I'm coming tonight."

It was the day after this that Glahn received the letter. That is to say, there came an express letter to him from the river station, it had made a detour of one hundred and eighty miles. The letter was written in a woman's hand, and I thought to myself that maybe it was from his former friend, the high-ranking lady. Glahn laughed nervously when he had read it and gave the delivery boy an extra bill for bringing it. But it wasn't long before he grew taciturn and gloomy, doing nothing but staring into vacancy. In the evening he got drunk, with an old dwarf of a native and his son, and he embraced me as well and insisted I drink with them.

"You're so amiable tonight," I said.[47]

Then he gave a very loud laugh and said, "Here the two of us spend our time in the middle of India shooting game, right? Terribly funny, isn't it? Here's to all the kingdoms and countries of the world, and to all beautiful women, married or unmarried, far and near. Haw-haw! Just think of it, a married woman proposing to a man, a married woman!"

"A countess!" I said sarcastically. I said it very sarcastically, and it hurt. He whined like a dog because it hurt. Then he suddenly wrinkled his brows and began blinking his eyes, pondering whether he might not have said too much, so solemnly did he act about that little secret of his. But just then some children came running up to our hut, yelling and screaming, "The tigers, halloa, the tigers!" A child had been snapped up by a tiger not far from the village, in a thicket between the village and the river.

That was enough for Glahn, who was drunk and whose mind was torn by grief. He grabbed his rifle and ran down to the thicket in a trice; he didn't even have a hat on his head. But why did he take his rifle instead of his shotgun, if he really was that brave? He had to wade across the river, which was not without danger, except that the river was almost dry at this time, before the rainy season. A while later I heard two shots and immediately afterward a third shot. Three shots for one animal! I thought; a lion would have fallen after two shots, and this is just a tiger! But even those three shots were to no purpose, the child was still torn to pieces and half devoured by the time Glahn got there; if he hadn't been so drunk, he wouldn't even have made an attempt to save it.

He spent the night living it up in the hut next door, with a widow and her two daughters—God only knows with which of them.

For two days Glahn wasn't sober for a single moment, and he had also picked up many companions to drink with. He urged me in vain to join in the binge, he no longer cared what he said and reproached me with being jealous of him.

"Your jealousy makes you blind," he said.

My jealousy! Me jealous of him!

"Really, now," I said, "jealous of you! What would I be jealous of you for?"

"All right, so you're not jealous of me," he replied. "By the way, I said hello to Maggie this evening, she was chewing as usual."

I swallowed my answer and left.

IV

We began to go out hunting again. Glahn felt he had wronged me and apologized.

"Anyway, I'm sick and tired of the whole thing," he said. "I just wish you'd miss the mark one day and plant a bullet in my throat."[48] The letter from the Countess may have been smoldering in his memory again, and I replied, "You've made your bed, so now you can lie in it."

He grew more reticent and gloomy with each passing day, he didn't drink anymore or say another word; his cheeks became hollow.

One day I suddenly heard chatting and laughter outside my
window; I glanced out—Glahn had again his merry look and
was talking to Maggie in a loud voice. He was using all his
charming ways with her. Maggie must have come straight from
home and Glahn had been on the lookout for her. They even
made no bones about getting together directly in front of my
window.

I felt a tremor in all my limbs, I cocked my rifle but[49] let
the hammer down again. I stepped out on the square and took
Maggie by the arm; we walked through the village in silence.
Glahn at once disappeared into the hut.

"Why are you speaking to him again?" I asked Maggie.

She didn't answer.

I was in mortal despair, my heart beating so hard I could
scarcely breathe. Never had I seen Maggie looking more beautiful; I had never seen an all-white girl who was that beautiful,
and therefore I forgot that she was a Tamil, I forgot everything
for her sake.

"Answer me," I said, "why do you speak to him?"

"I like him better," she said.

"You like him better than me?"

"Yes."

All right, she liked him better, though I bet I could hold
my own against him! Hadn't I always been kind to her and
given her money and presents? And what had he done?

"He makes fun of you, he says you're chewing things," I said.

That she failed to understand, and so I explained to her that
she was in the habit of putting all sorts of things in her mouth and
chewing them, and that Glahn poked fun at her for it. This made
more of an impression on her than anything else that I said.

"Look here, Maggie," I went on, "you shall be mine for-
ever, wouldn't you like that! I've been thinking it over, you
shall come with me when I go away from here. Listen, I want
to marry you, and we'll go to my own country and live there.
You would like that, wouldn't you?"

And this also made an impression on her, Maggie grew vivacious and talked a lot to me on our walk. Only once did she mention Glahn, asking, "And will Glahn come with us when we go away?"

"No," I replied, "he won't. Do you feel sad about that?"

"No, no," she replied quickly, "I feel glad about it."

That was all she said about him, and I felt reassured. Maggie also came home with me when I asked her to.

When she left me a couple of hours later, I climbed up the ladder to Glahn's room and knocked on the thin reed door. He was home. I said, "I've come to tell you that perhaps we shouldn't go hunting tomorrow."

"Why not?" Glahn asked.

"Because I can't guarantee I won't miss the mark, that I won't plant a bullet in your throat."

Glahn didn't answer and I went down again. After that warning he probably wouldn't dare go hunting in the morning. But why, then, had he lured Maggie below my window and flirted loudly with her? Why didn't he go back home again, if the letter really summoned him back? Instead, he would often clench his teeth and shout apropos of nothing, "Never! Never! I'd rather be drawn and quartered!"

And still, the morning after I had given him that warning Glahn stood before my bed and cried, "Up, up, comrade! It's a most lovely day, we've got to shoot something. Anyway, what you said last night was very silly."

It wasn't even past four, but I got up at once and made ready to go along, because he had scorned my warning. I loaded my gun before setting out and let him stand and watch me doing it. Anyway, it was not a most lovely day, as he had said; it was raining, and this compounded his mockery. But I put a good face on it and went along with him without a word.

We roamed about in the forest all day, each with his own thoughts. We didn't shoot anything, missing out on one quarry after another because we were thinking of other things than the hunt. Around noon Glahn began walking some way ahead of me, as if he wanted to give me a better opportunity of doing with him what I wished. He walked directly in front of the muzzle of my gun, but I also endured this insult. We returned home in the evening without anything having happened. I thought to myself, Maybe he'll watch his step now and leave Maggie alone!

"This has been the longest day of my life," Glahn said that evening as we were standing by the hut.

Nothing more was said between us.

The next few days he was in the blackest humor, no doubt still on account of that letter. "I just cannot stand it, no, I cannot stand it!" he would say from time to time in the night; we could hear it all through the hut. He carried his sulkiness to the point of not answering even the friendliest questions of our landlady, and what's more, he moaned in his sleep. He must have a lot on his conscience, I thought; but why in the world does he not go home? His arrogance forbade him, no doubt: once having been refused, he would not be the one who came back.

I met Maggie every evening, and Glahn no longer talked to her. I noticed that she had stopped chewing, she didn't chew at all anymore, and I was happy about that and thought, She isn't chewing things anymore, that's one fault less, and I love her twice as much as before! One day she asked about Glahn, she asked very cautiously. Was he not well? Had he gone away?

"If he's not dead or gone," I replied, "he's probably lying at home. It's all the same to me. He has become quite insufferable."

But when we reached the hut just then, we spotted Glahn stretched out on a mat on the ground, his hands clasped behind his neck, staring up at the sky.

"Anyway, there he is," I said.

Maggie went straight up to him before I could stop her and said in a cheerful voice, "I'm not chewing things anymore, see for yourself! No feathers, no coins, no bits of paper, nothing at all!"

Glahn barely glanced at her and continued to lie still; Maggie and I left. When I reproached her for breaking her promise and speaking to Glahn again, she replied she had only wanted to reprimand him.

"Yes, that's good, do reprimand him," I said. "But it wasn't for his sake you stopped chewing things, was it?"

She didn't answer. What, did she refuse to answer?

"Do you hear? Tell me, was it for his sake?"

"No, no," she then replied, "it was for your sake."

Nor could I believe otherwise. Why should she do anything for Glahn's sake?

That evening Maggie promised to come to me, and she did.

V

She came at ten o'clock, I could hear her voice outside, she was talking loudly to a child whom she led by the hand. Why did she not come in, and why had she brought the child? As I watch her, something tells me she is giving a signal by talking so loud to the child; I also notice that she keeps her eyes turned toward the attic, toward Glahn's window. Had he nodded to her perhaps, or waved from behind the window when he heard her talking outside? In any case, I understood enough to know that one does not need to look up at the sky when speaking to a child on the ground.

I was on the point of going out to her and taking her by the arm; however, just then she let go of the child's hand, leaving the child standing there, while she herself went in through the door of the hut. She stepped into the hallway. Well, there she was at last, I would let her have it when she came!

I can hear Maggie stepping into the hallway, there's no mistake, she is almost at my door. But instead of coming into my room, she climbs up to the attic, to Glahn's hole, I can hear her footsteps on the ladder, I can hear it all too well. I push my door wide open, but Maggie is already up there. The door closes

· behind her and I hear nothing more. That was at ten o'clock.

I go into my own room and sit down, pick up my gun and load it, though it is in the middle of the night. At twelve o'clock I climb up the ladder and listen at Glahn's door; I can hear Maggie in there, I can hear her being sweet to Glahn and get down again. At one o'clock, when I climb back up, all is quiet. I wait outside the door until they awake. It gets to be three, it gets to be four; at five they woke up. Good! I thought to myself; and I thought of nothing but the fact that they were now awake and that that was very good. But shortly afterward I heard some noise and disturbance downstairs, in my landlady's room, and I had to get down again in a hurry not to have her take me by surprise. Glahn and Maggie were clearly awake and I could have eavesdropped to much more, but I had to go.

In the hallway I said to myself, See, here she went, brushing my door with her arm, but she did not open the door, she went up the ladder; and here is the ladder, her footprints are on these four steps.[50]

My bed had still not been slept in, nor did I lie down now; I sat down by the window, fiddling with my rifle. My heart did not beat, it throbbed.

Half an hour later I once more hear Maggie's footsteps on the ladder. Leaning over against the window, I see her walk out of the hut. She was wearing that short little cotton skirt which didn't even reach to her knees, and over her shoulders a woolen scarf she had borrowed from Glahn. Apart from that she was completely naked, and her little cotton skirt was very crumpled. She walked slowly, as she was in the habit of doing, without as much as a glance up at my window even now. Then she disappeared among the huts.

A while later Glahn came down, rifle under his arm, all ready to go hunting. He looked gloomy and didn't wish me good morning. However, he had spruced himself up and taken exceptional care with his toilet. He has adorned himself like a bridegroom, I thought.

I got ready at once and went with him, and neither of us said a word. The first two partridges we shot were a sorry torn-up mess because we shot them with our rifles, but we roasted them under a tree as best we could and consumed them in silence. Then time went by till twelve o'clock.

Glahn called out to me, "Are you sure you have loaded? We might run across something unexpected. Load just in case."

"I have loaded," I answered back.

Then he disappeared behind a thicket for a moment. What pleasure it would be to shoot him, gun him down like a dog! There was no hurry, he could still regale himself with the thought of it; for he obviously understood what I had in mind, that was why he asked if I had loaded. Not even today had he been able to forbear indulging his insolent pride, having spruced himself up and put on a new shirt; he had an excessively proud air about him.

Around one o'clock he stops in front of me, pale and angry, and says, "Why, I cannot stand it! Do check if you have loaded, man, if you've got anything in your gun!"

"If you please, look after your own gun!" I replied. But I knew very well why he was constantly asking about my gun.

And again he walked away from me. My answer had rebuffed him so emphatically that he grew meek, hanging his head as he walked away.

A moment later I shot a pigeon and reloaded. While I am busy with this, Glahn stands half hidden behind a tree trunk watching me, watching to see if I am really loading; shortly after he starts singing a hymn, loud and clear—a bridal hymn, at that. He sings bridal hymns and puts on his Sunday best, I thought to myself, that's his way of trying to be at his most charming today. Before he had even finished singing, he began walking slowly in front of me, hanging his head and still singing as he walked. Again he kept directly in front of the muzzle of my rifle, as if he were thinking, There, now it will come to pass, that's why I'm singing this bridal hymn! But nothing came to pass yet, and when he fell silent he had to look back at me.

"We won't shoot anything today in any case," he said and smiled, by way of apologizing and making amends for singing while out hunting. Even at that moment his smile was beautiful, it was as though he were weeping inwardly; and, in fact, his lips were trembling, although he plumed himself on being able to smile at such a solemn moment.

I was no woman, and he must have noticed that he was making no impression on me. Grown impatient, pale, he circled around me with furious steps, now to the left of me, now to the right, stopping to wait for me every once in a while. Around five o'clock I suddenly heard a crack, and a bullet whistled past my left ear. Looking up, I saw Glahn standing motionless a few paces away staring at me, his smoking rifle on his arm. Had he tried to shoot me? I said, "You missed, you've been a poor shot lately."

But he was not a poor shot, he never missed, he had only wanted to provoke me.

"Then take your revenge and be damned!" he screamed back.

"When my time is come," I said, clenching my teeth.

We stand there eyeing one another, and suddenly Glahn shrugs his shoulders and cries "Coward!" at me. Why should he call me a coward? I slammed my rifle to my cheek, aimed straight at his face and pulled the trigger.

You've made your bed, so now you can lie in it. . . .

But now the Glahn family need no longer look for this man; it continues to irritate me to come across this idiotic advertisement offering such and such a reward for information about a dead man. Thomas Glahn died in an accident, killed by an accidental shot while hunting in India. The court put away his name and the manner of his death in a register with corded leaves, and in that register it says that he is dead, I tell you, even that he died the victim of a stray bullet.

EXPLANATORY NOTES

3 *Nordland:* In the strict sense, the name of the county that includes most of the long neck of the Norwegian land mass. It extends south–north for about three hundred miles and is bisected by the Arctic Circle. In casual usage, it is taken to mean North Norway in general.

5 *Sirilund:* Hamsun's trading center seems to be based on Kjerringøy, located about twenty miles north of the town of Bodø and roughly midway between the Arctic Circle and Narvik. Its local business magnate in Hamsun's youth, the period that seems to be reflected in the story—the early 1870s rather than the indicated 1850s—was the wealthy merchant, banker and philanthropist E. B. K. Zahl (1826–1900). As an aspiring young writer, Hamsun had received financial assistance from Zahl.

6 *Mr. Mack:* This figure, who appears in several novels by Knut Hamsun, possesses some of the characteristics of an Oriental potentate or a feudal lord of the Middle Ages. His extraordinary power, which turns him into a kind of ruler of Sirilund, depends on his virtually absolute control of the region's economic life. Mack is believed by many to be modeled on the above-mentioned benefactor of young Hamsun, E. B. K. Zahl.

17 *Carl Johan's own hands:* King Carl Johan, born Jean-Baptiste Jules Bernadotte, began his career as a French Revolutionary general and served as a minister of war under Napoleon. Later he turned against the Emperor and helped defeat him at Leipzig (1813). After being chosen Swedish crown prince, he forced Denmark, which had sided with Napoleon, to cede Norway to Sweden. Carl Johan (Charles John or Charles XIV) ruled the joint kingdom of Norway-Sweden from 1818 to 1844.

19 *Diderik and Iselin:* Diderik and Iselin and the other legendary figures seem to belong exclusively to Hamsun's fictional universe. In *Munken Vendt* (1902), a dramatic poem or verse drama set in the eighteenth century, these figures appear as real-life characters.

65 *Spitsbergen:* The largest island of Svalbard, a Norwegian possession in the Arctic Ocean.

65–66 *Baron:* Said to be a Finlander, the Baron is most likely intended to be a Swedo-Finn. Finland was politically dominated by Sweden from the twelfth century on. With varying degrees of control, this dominance was maintained until 1809, when Finland was ceded to Russia. However, Finland had—and continues to have—a sizable Swedish-language minority.

70 *Xanthus:* According to tradition, Xanthus was not Aesop's teacher but his master. Aesop was a slave for many years.

The fact that this incident is reported indirectly makes one wonder how complete Glahn's narrative is supposed to be. A later novel by Hamsun, *Rosa* (1908), suggests that Glahn did not tell the whole story of his relationship with Edvarda. For example, in chapter eight of that book Edvarda—now a widow with two children—relates to Parelius, the young narrator, several incidents from her adventure with Glahn not covered in *Pan*, including an abortive suicide pact.

81 *Iron Nights:* Thought to be the time when killing frost first occurred in the northern latitudes where the story takes place.

84 *blind old Lapp:* Though the ethnic group referred to here now mostly goes by the name Sami, Lapp (or Laplander) conforms to the English usage at the time of the novel's action.

91 *Dragon—Argus:* Here the Doctor's teasing of Edvarda gives one pause. Argus, the hundred-eyed monster set by jealous Hera to guard Io after Zeus had turned her into a heifer, seems quite correct. The Doctor may be alluding to Ladon, the hundred-headed dragon who guarded the golden apples of the Hesperides, or to Fafnir, who guarded the treasure of the Nibelungs.

91 *conditions in the Crimea:* The reference is to the Crimean War (1853–56), between Russia and the allied powers of Turkey, England, France and Sardinia. Today the war is probably remembered mostly for the nursing and hospital reforms of Florence Nightingale (1820–1910).

91 *Napoleon:* This is Napoleon III (1808–1873), Emperor of France 1852–70. During the Crimean War he restored French leadership on the Continent.

TEXTUAL NOTES

The language of the first edition of *Pan* looks very much like Danish. The changes that were made in subsequent editions were partly formal, partly substantive. The spelling and grammar were Norwegianized, as was some of the vocabulary. Though the substantive changes are less extensive than those in Hamsun's first two novels, *Hunger* (1890) and *Mysteries* (1892), they deserve to be noted. However, many minor alterations have not been included in the tabulation below.

Since there exists no authoritative edition of Hamsun's works, I have followed the first edition wherever it seemed superior to the latest collected one. All such instances have been indicated in the notes.

The first edition, published by P. G. Philipsen (Copenhagen, 1894) and, in facsimile, by Gyldendal (Oslo, 1994), will in these notes be indicated by "P," the collected edition (Knut Hamsun, *Samlede verker*, vol. 2 [Oslo: Gyldendal, 1992]) by "CW." The page references to P are listed first.

1. 2/333. P reads: *a single night was enough to make them come out in all their glory,*
2. 10/336. Here I follow P in using comma rather than period.
3. 10/336. The intensive *so* in P (after "opens") was deleted in CW.
4. 17/339. The phrase *on the rocks* was added in CW.
5. 22/341. Deleted in CW: *yes, quite like tenderness,*
6. 22/341. Here I follow the syntax of P, making the clause *as I entered the hut* dependent on the first rather than the last main clause.
7. 35/346. In P the word here used refers to an undergarment, best rendered as *shift*.
8. 35/346. Here P repeats *Iselin.*
9. 36/346. In starting a new section here I follow P.
10. 37/347. To reinforce the passage of time, I follow P in separating the last sentence from the dialogue by extra space.
11. 39/347. *After all* and the question mark at the end of the sentence were added in CW.
12. 42/348. The last phrase was added in CW.

13. 45/350. In starting a new section here I follow P.

14. 58/355. The word *erotic* (or sexual) was added in CW.

15. 58/355. In starting a new section here I follow P.

16. 67/358. The entire last sentence (from "If she then had answered") was added in CW.

17. 70/359. The phrase *and then looked away again* was added in CW.

18. 73/360. In P, the last clause reads, *it is a remembrance.*

19. 75/361. The phrase *filled with water and* was added in CW.

20. 80/363. Here P contains an intensifying phrase, *oh, more than I could,* deleted from CW.

21. 114/376. In starting a new section here I follow P.

22. 115/376. Here and in the preceding sentence the intensifying adverb *so* before "afraid" was deleted in CW.

23. 127/381. Here I follow P rather than CW, which reads *One evening . . .*

24. 127/381. The phrase *to be discourteous* was added in CW.

25. 128/381. The phrase *as weather signs* was added in CW.

26. 130/382. In P the modifier to "forehead" is *dark.*

27. 137/385. In starting a new section here I follow P.

28. 137/385. The clause *because I don't accept the kerchief* was added in CW.

29. 147/389. In using italics here I follow P.

30. 148/389. Instead of "pure," P has *dear.*

31. 154/391. In starting a new section here I follow P.

32. 154/391. The phrase *among the trees* was added in CW.

33. 155/392. The sentence *she pretended she didn't know me* was added in CW.

34. 158/393. Here I follow P in *not* starting a new section.

35. 158/393. The clause *when I come,* which followed "tomorrow" in P, was deleted in CW.

36. 159/393. In P, this sentence reads simply *the night is deep.*

37. 159/394. In omitting the conjunction "and" at this point, I follow P.

38. 165/396. This sentence was added in CW.

39. 167/396. This sentence was added in CW.

40. 171/398. The preceding sentence was added in CW.

41. 173/399. The word *probably* was added in CW.

42. 175/400. The last two sentences were added in CW.

43. 205/410. This sentence was added in CW.

44. 206/410. The clause *go and hunt up lots of people* was added in CW.
45. 206/410. In starting a new section here I follow P.
46. 222/416. At this point CW has a one-sentence paragraph, *"You're so amiable tonight," I said.* This is obviously a mistake. See the following note.
47. 224/416. In placing the above remark here, I am following P.
48. 227/417. At this point P starts a new paragraph. It reads: *These were the sort of thoughts he harbored, that I should plant a bullet in his throat,* followed by "The letter from the Countess . . ."
49. 228/418. In using *but* rather than "and" (as in CW) here, I am following P.
50. 237/421. In starting a new paragraph here I follow P.

FOR THE BEST IN PAPERBACKS, LOOK FOR THE 🐧

In every corner of the world, on every subject under the sun, Penguin represents quality and variety—the very best in publishing today.

For complete information about books available from Penguin—including Puffins, Penguin Classics, and Compass—and how to order them, write to us at the appropriate address below. Please note that for copyright reasons the selection of books varies from country to country.

In the United Kingdom: Please write to *Dept. EP, Penguin Books Ltd, Bath Road, Harmondsworth, West Drayton, Middlesex UB7 0DA.*

In the United States: Please write to *Penguin Putnam Inc., P.O. Box 12289 Dept. B, Newark, New Jersey 07101-5289* or call 1-800-788-6262.

In Canada: Please write to *Penguin Books Canada Ltd, 10 Alcorn Avenue, Suite 300, Toronto, Ontario M4V 3B2.*

In Australia: Please write to *Penguin Books Australia Ltd, P.O. Box 257, Ringwood, Victoria 3134.*

In New Zealand: Please write to *Penguin Books (NZ) Ltd, Private Bag 102902, North Shore Mail Centre, Auckland 10.*

In India: Please write to *Penguin Books India Pvt Ltd, 11 Panchsheel Shopping Centre, Panchsheel Park, New Delhi 110 017.*

In the Netherlands: Please write to *Penguin Books Netherlands bv, Postbus 3507, NL-1001 AH Amsterdam.*

In Germany: Please write to *Penguin Books Deutschland GmbH, Metzlerstrasse 26, 60594 Frankfurt am Main.*

In Spain: Please write to *Penguin Books S. A., Bravo Murillo 19, 1° B, 28015 Madrid.*

In Italy: Please write to *Penguin Italia s.r.l., Via Benedetto Croce 2, 20094 Corsico, Milano.*

In France: Please write to *Penguin France, Le Carré Wilson, 62 rue Benjamin Baillaud, 31500 Toulouse.*

In Japan: Please write to *Penguin Books Japan Ltd, Kaneko Building, 2-3-25 Koraku, Bunkyo-Ku, Tokyo 112.*

In South Africa: Please write to *Penguin Books South Africa (Pty) Ltd, Private Bag X14, Parkview, 2122 Johannesburg.*